**He's a ticking**

**Eric Trask** is counting the days before he blasts out of Shaw's Crossing forever. He and his brothers were raised at GodsAcre, a mysterious doomsday cult deep in the mountains, and are the only survivors of the deadly fire that destroyed it. The townspeople see them as time bombs just waiting to blow, but Eric's going to prove those bastards wrong. He's an ex-Marine, fresh off a tour in Afghanistan, working three jobs and barely sleeping. Utterly unprepared for Demi Vaughan's dazzling green eyes, lush pink lips and sexy curves. She's the town princess…he's a dangerous outcast. It was a sure recipe for disaster.

But the closer he gets to Demi, the more impossible it is to resist…

**Forbidden fruit is the sweetest…**

**Demi Vaughan** has big plans for life post- college, and Eric Trask, notorious bad boy with a complicated past, is not part of them. So when he saunters into the sandwich shop where she works she tells herself he's just tall, ripped, smoldering eye candy, nothing more. Eric was damaged. Marked by violence and tragedy. He'd be the ultimate bad boyfriend, and right now she was too busy even to shop for a good one. But his hot eyes and hard body, his sensual smile and that rough, sexy voice of his shook her resolve. After all, she was leaving this place forever. A little taste of heaven…what could it hurt?

But Shaw's Crossing has deeper, darker secrets than Eric or Demi could guess. The evil that destroyed GodsAcre is lying in wait...**and it will stop at nothing to keep Eric and Demi apart…**

**Visit me at my website, http://shannonmckenna.com for news and updates, but the best way to stay in touch is to subscribe to my newsletter! Here's the link, http://shannonmckenna.com/connect.php, so you'll never miss a new book or a great promo! Plus, look out for a special gift from me to subscribers…a free Obsidian Files novel!**

THE HELLBOUND BROTHERHOOD
BOOK ONE

SHANNON McKENNA

# PRAISE FOR SHANNON McKENNA

“Blends an intensely terrifying psychic thriller with a mind-blowing erotic romance.”
—**Library Journal**, on *Fade To Midnight*

“Blasts readers with a highly charged, action-adventure romance . . . extra steamy.”
—**Booklist**

“Pulse-pounding . . . with searing sex and raw emotions.”
—**Romantic Times**, 4 ½ stars

“Shannon McKenna makes the pulse pound.”
—**Bookpage**

“Shannon McKenna introduces us to fleshed-out characters in a tailspin plot that culminates in an explosive ending.”
—**Fresh Fiction**

"An erotic romance in a suspense vehicle on overdrive . . . sizzles!”
—**RT Book Reviews**

"McKenna expertly stokes the fires of romantic tension."
—**Publishers Weekly**

"McKenna strikes gold again."
—**Publishers Weekly**

"Her books will take readers on a nonstop thrill ride and leave them begging for more when the last pages are devoured."
—**Maya Banks**, *New York Times* bestselling author

"Full of turbocharged sex scenes, this action-packed novel is sure to be a crowd pleaser."
—**Publishers Weekly** on *Edge Of Midnight*

"Highly creative . . . erotic sex and constant danger."
—**Romantic Times** on *Hot Night* (4 ½-star review and a Top Pick)

"Aims for the heart with scorching precision."
—**Publishers Weekly** *on Ultimate Weapon*

# ALSO BY SHANNON McKENNA

**The Hellbound Brotherhood**

*Hellion*

*Headlong*

**The Obsidian Files Series**

*Right Through Me*

*My Next Breath*

*In My Skin*

*Light Me Up*

**The McClouds & Friends Series**

*Behind Closed Doors*

*Standing In The Shadows*

*Out Of Control*

*Edge Of Midnight*

*Extreme Danger*

*Ultimate Weapon*

*Fade To Midnight*

*Blood And Fire*

*One Wrong Move*

*Fatal Strike*

*In For The Kill*

**Stand-alone Titles**

*Return To Me*

*Hot Night*

*Tasting Fear*

**Anthologies**

*All Through The Night*

(with Suzanne Forster, Thea Devine and Lori Foster)

*I Brake For Bad Boys*

(with Lori Foster and Janelle Denison)

*Bad Boys Next Exit*

(with Donna Kauffman and E.C. Sheedy)

*Baddest Bad Boys*

(with E.C. Sheedy and Cate Noble)

*All About Men*

(a single author anthology)

http://shannonmckenna.com

Print ISBN: 978-0-9977941-8-2
Digital ISBN: 978-0-9977941-9-9

# 1

Demi didn't need to turn around from the frozen yogurt machine to know that Eric had made his grand entrance. The muffled squeals and excited whispering from the other girls behind the Bakery Café's counter gave it away. Lame-brains. They'd been teasing her about that guy for weeks. Ever since he started coming in here for lunch.

Yes, folks, Eric Trask had entered the building.

Even if she didn't look around, the effect on her was the same. The ambient temperature shot up ten degrees, *whoosh*. The earth shifted on its axis, *ka-chunk*.

Crap. Blushing again. Rosy red right down to the edge of her tee-shirt. Her damn cleavage was blushing.

*Stop this bullshit. He's a cute guy. Eye candy. Not earth-shattering.*

The frozen yogurt overflowed the cup and glopped out onto her hand.

Demi cleaned up the mess and sidled over to the crushed Oreos and colored sprinkles without turning around. She was playing it cool. She had no idea he was there. Who? She didn't even notice him. Why should she? She was working. Busy, busy Demi. Working toward her goals. She couldn't be bothered with this nonsense. She had no time to waste with—*ouch.*

She'd smacked her hip on the corner of the ice-cream toppings table.

Eric Trask loomed in her peripheral vision as she deposited the frozen yogurt on the tray full of sandwiches. She made change and smiling chit-chat, having no idea what she was saying. Executive function in her brain was totally AWOL.

He hung back from the counter, ostensibly studying the sandwich board while he waited until she was free to wait on him. Kaia and Tammi leaned over the counter, their boobs practically spilling out of their shirts in their eagerness to take his order.

"Can I help you?" Tammi sang out.

"Still thinking, thanks," he replied, eyes fixed on the menu.

*Ahhhh.* His deep voice was scratchy and rough. More smothered giggling from Tammi and Kaia. *Grow the fuck up, ladies.*

Demi finally allowed herself to look. She had to work up to it slowly, the experience being a full frontal assault on her senses.

He was ridiculously tall, to start with. At least six-three. Broad, too, but lean and tapered. He looked dusty and hot, his tee-shirt stretching deliciously tight over the defined muscle bulges. She loved the way his sleeves strained over the swell of his biceps. She wanted to run her fingers over every contour. Nature's ultimate sculpture.

Hoo boy. It was a struggle to keep her mouth firmly closed.

His dark blond hair had sported a jarhead buzz-cut before, as befitted a Marine recently back from his second tour of duty in Afghanistan, but it was starting to get a little shaggy on top. His face still had that deep, weathered desert tan. His eyes were a piercing pale gray against his sun-browned skin, like glints of shining chrome. The eye-crinkles around them made him look older than his twenty-four years. Two years older than her.

His eyes had always made him look older. She'd noticed it back in high school, from the first moment she laid eyes on him. He'd been sixteen, she'd been fourteen. He hadn't noticed her. He'd seen too many things he was desperate to forget. The GodsAcre story was blood-chilling, and people never got tired of chewing over it.

That sadness in his eyes had given her a hot, shaky feeling even then. It had made something inside her chest become soft, achy. Made something melt that should have stayed solid.

She wasn't the only one melting for the Trask boys. With their muscular good looks, daydreaming about them became a widespread recreational pastime for all the girls at Shaw's Crossing High School, in spite of the stories about the crazy mountain cult where they grew up. According to the gossip, GodsAcre had been a hotbed of drugs, brain-washing, sex orgies, Satanism. It was even whispered that the Trask brothers were psycho killers trained by Delta Force soldier Jeremiah Paley, GodsAcre's leader, also known as 'The Prophet.' That the three brothers had set the fire that had destroyed GodsAcre themselves.

So. There were possible mass murderers, sitting right there with the rest of them, taking notes in AP Chemistry or Spanish or English class just like normal teenagers.

Normal aside from the fact that they were considerably hotter, that is.

Her granddad had been horrified when his old Marine buddy and longtime friend, Police Chief Otis Trask, had announced his intention of taking in the GodsAcre boys. They needed a home, Otis had argued. They needed to stay together. It was dangerous to leave them to themselves, and Otis didn't see anyone else stepping up.

Bad idea. Everyone said so. Those boys belonged in a reformatory. Granddad had tried so hard to dissuade Otis, anyone listening would have thought the three boys were fire-breathing demons from hell. Demi remembered him ranting about how damaged and maladapted they must be. How irresponsible it was for the school to let them mix with normal kids after their bizarre upbringing. How it was begging for disaster.

But Otis held firm. The boys moved in with him, and enrolled in the high school.

Crazy rumors hadn't stopped her from staring at Eric whenever she got the chance. His cheekbones, his broad shoulders, his strong jaw, his sensual lips. He was even handsomer now than he had been back in high school. Bigger, taller, thicker, harder.

His gorgeous smile had become a grin. His teeth were so white. Deep smile grooves cut into his lean cheeks. Like dimples, but longer.

"...everything okay?" He sounded like he was repeating himself. She could feel the heat coming off his body.

Damn. That mind-wiping storm wind of testosterone was putting her into a fugue state. She forced herself to breathe. Air helped.

"Ah…ah, yes. Of course. I'm fine." She smiled back at him. "What'll it be?" She hoped that she hadn't already asked him that. Perhaps even gotten an answer.

That grin widened. "Surprise me."

"Is that a challenge?"

"Yeah."

She looked down her nose at him. A neat trick, at five-foot-four. It took lots of attitude, tiptoes, and hiking her chin way up high. "Game on."

Kaia sidled past Demi as she grabbed a couple of slices of rye bread and headed to the sandwich bar. "Surprise me?" she said under her breath. "I'd surprise that guy right out of his clothes. Any time, any place."

"Make that sandwich really tall, girl," Tammi cooed as she swept by with a drinks order. "And don't skimp the sauce. You want it really juicy, so that that thick wad of hot, salty meat can slip right down, you know what I'm talking about?"

"Shut…*up!*" Demi whispered savagely.

"What do you think, Kai?" Tammi said to Kaia. "Mayo? Or herb vinaigrette?"

"Oh, ranch, for sure. Long, strong squirts of it."

"Piss off, both of you," Demi snapped. "I'm busy."

"I just bet you are, you lucky girl."

Demi blocked them out of her consciousness by concentrating on making the sandwich for the ages. One worthy of fueling a body that gorgeous. Rye bread, grilled in herbed dill butter, piled with pepper rolled roast beef and thick slabs of melted pepper-jack cheese. A few draped pieces roasted red pepper, juicy slices of crimson heirloom tomatoes, some tender green Bibb lettuce. A towering stack of home fried potatoes and a scoop of her own specially tweaked coleslaw. A bottle of an herbal tea and fruit infusion.

"Don't forget the pickle, girlfriend," Tammi sang out. "A nice, fat one."

Demi gave her the finger over her shoulder as she bopped the swinging door open with her hip and carried out the tray with her creation on it. Not blushing this time, oh no. She'd been slaving over a hot griddle. She got that tomato-red color from honest toil and no one could say she hadn't.

She laid the sandwich down in front of him. "Here you go. A Demi Vaughan special. Billed by the till as a roast beef and cheese, but I tarted it up for you. And a green tea, lime and goji berry cocktail to wash it down. It'll balance your heart chakra, flood you with antioxidants and replace lost electrolytes."

His silver-chrome eyes flicked up and down her body. "Looks incredible." His deep, throaty rasp brushed tenderly on every nerve. "Thanks for keeping it special. My heart chakra is getting all excited just from looking at it."

She smiled, fishing for something cute and witty to say. Came up blank.

He started again. "Hey, I just wanted to ask you—"

"Demi!" Raelene, her boss, hollered from kitchen, cutting off his words. "Demi, get back here for a second!"

"Be right there." She backed awkwardly away before she realized what she was doing and turned around to walk away with some dignity. Like a normal human being.

In the kitchen, Raelene, a skinny lady with a graying crown of braids, handed her a clipboard. "I want you to do some inventory in the storeroom," she announced.

"Inventory?" Demi glanced back toward Eric before she could stop herself.

Raelene caught the look. "Tammi or Kaia can ring him up. You'll need to do boring crap busywork when you're running your own business, you know. Get used to it."

"Of course, but during the lunch rush?"

"I'll help the other girls up front if they need it. And I know it's not my business, but that boy is a dead end. Don't conduct your flirtations on my clock, Demi."

Demi bristled. "I'm not! I have never wasted time on the job."

Raelene's mouth tightened. "Stay away from him. He's bad luck. Bad news."

"It's nobody's business, and I don't see why you would even—"

"The Prophet's Curse got my brother. Did you know that?"

Demi stared at the older woman, appalled. "Raelene. Please. You don't mean you actually believe those old rumors? That's just a vicious, crazy story. An urban myth."

Raelene shrugged. "Fourteen people dead in twelve days," she said. "And it happened right after Darryl refused to give Jeremiah another building permit for his compound. The old bastard wanted to build right in the middle of an elk run. Darryl said no. And the next day, he was dead. Is that an urban myth, you think?"

"Natural causes," Demi said.

"Right," Raelene said. "Like all the rest of the people the Prophet was pissed with. That's a whole lot of natural causes crowded together in a very small time frame. A very small geographical area. Too small."

"But…you think Darryl was poisoned?" Demi said

hesitantly. "Or are you saying that it's an actual curse? Like, black magic, or something? You're not serious."

She studied the other woman's face. The realization dawned slowly, with a sickening chill.

Raelene was dead serious.

"Raelene," Demi said. "Even if Darryl really was murdered somehow, and even if it actually was Jeremiah's fault, he's dead and gone. It wasn't Eric or his brothers who caused any of that stuff to happen. They were only kids at the time. It can't be their fault."

"I didn't say it was their fault," Raelene said stiffly. "I don't understand what happened back then, but it was sick and bad, and I don't like to see a nice young lady getting mixed up with it. Neither would your mother, as I'm sure you know."

Demi felt her back prickle. "He's not a criminal, Raelene. He's a veteran, he works, he's not in any kind of trouble, so I don't understand why you—"

"We're not having this conversation on my dime. Get to work if you still want this job. If you don't, you know where the door is."

Raelene marched out of the kitchen, rubber-soled trainers squeaking aggressively.

Demi was speechless. Her first instinct was to walk out. Screw this crap. Raelene had no right to preach or pass judgment about Demi's private life and personal choices.

But she couldn't afford to throw a tantrum. Her parents were already angry and disappointed with her. They'd been angry ever since she changed her major to restaurant management, rather than business administration, and they got even angrier when she refused the internship at the Shaw Paper Products distribution center in Tacoma. Or at any of the other SPP centers scattered over the western US, for that matter.

Dad had used his most sneering tone. *The little princess is too good for the family business? You'd rather wait tables and carry catering trays than take a shot at a grown-up job? A sandwich shop is your goddamn life's ambition now?*

She'd hoped for a summer job in her field for those last few weeks before her internship in Seattle started. The internship was a hard-won prize, and she could hardly wait to start. Eight weeks working closely with famed chef Maurizio Altamura at the renowned restaurant *Peccati di Gola*. In the meantime, she wasn't too proud to sling hash at the Bakery Café in Shaw's Crossing. It was food prep, and therefore relevant to her future plans. Somewhat. And this way, she could save on rent for a few more weeks.

But her parents, and Granddad, had been horrified. So she couldn't bail on the Bakery Café the first time she got huffy with the boss. Not in her shaky position.

Demi resisted the urge to peek and see if Eric was still there. She couldn't let him see her do that. It would look desperate and fawning and childish.

Besides, he was probably back at work. Maybe drinking what was left of his green tea and goji berry cocktail. Maybe holding the cool, sweaty bottle up against his hot face. Putting it to his lush, sensual lips, throat working as he drank. Until a single drop of condensation from the bottle trickled slowly…sexily…down his strong, tanned throat.

Whew. One would think that the dull task of counting cans and bottles in a pantry would chill an overheated girl right down.

Think again.

# 2

Eric drove slowly past the sandwich shop for the fourth time.

He wasn't going back inside today. Not after the death-ray stare from Raelene Muir. He'd make problems for Demi. Probably already had. Looked like she'd been banished to the back room for the crime of speaking to him.

Raelene had kept up the sphincter-mouthed glare the whole time he was eating his sandwich. He was used to it, so it didn't affect his appetite, but damn, that shit got old.

He shouldn't be eating at the Bakery Café in any case. Dropping seventy bucks a week for fancy sandwiches and overpriced beverages was stupid right now. He was busting his ass to save money for developing his app, and he could make an entire week's worth of perfectly good lunch sandwiches for the cost of a single meal at that place.

But still, he kept going back. Just to ogle Demi Vaughan's sparkling green eyes and shapely ass. And those luscious, gravity-defying tits that made his fingers buzz with lustful curiosity. Her velvety alto voice made him sweat. He heard it in his dreams.

She acted like she could care less, but her hot blush gave her away.

Finally, she emerged. Boyd Nevins followed her out of the café. Boyd had gone to high school with them. He'd been in Eric's class. He'd heard that Boyd now worked for Demi's family's paper packing materials company over at Granger Valley.

Boyd was leaning in toward her, working his dimples. The guy was tall and blond. Good-looking, he guessed, and he could turn on the charm when he exerted himself. But Eric and his brothers knew first-hand that Boyd was a conniving shithead and bully. At least, he had been back in their school years.

Demi kept smiling and shaking her head, and Boyd kept talking. She backed away, still smiling. He grabbed her wrist, pulling her back toward him. Demi's smile faltered.

She tried to pull free. Boyd held on tight. Dickhead. He hadn't changed.

On impulse, Eric rolled down the passenger side window. Very carefully, to keep the damn thing from coming loose and falling down inside the car door, as it often did.

"Hey, Demi," he called. "Sorry I'm late. You ready to go?"

It was a risk, but giving her an escape hatch from Boyd was an opportunity he'd be an idiot not to take. Then again, if Boyd was a frying pan, she might think that Eric was the fire.

Demi's eyes flicked to him, blank and startled for a second. "Hey," she said back. "Ah…yes. Yes, I am, actually." She wrenched her arm free. "Later, Boyd."

Boyd glared at Eric as she got into his car. Eric gave him a big smile and pulled out into the street.

"Hope you didn't mind me pretending we had a date," he said. "I didn't like the way he yanked on your arm. Thought I'd give you an out."

"I was okay. Boyd isn't a problem for me. But I do appreciate the thought."

He took a deep breath and went for it. "Can I make our fake date a real one? We can grab something to drink. Iced coffee, a shake, a beer. Whatever you'd like."

Her rosy lips opened slightly and stayed open as her color deepened. "I'd love to, but I can't tonight. I promised to get dinner on for my mom. She's at the library board meeting tonight, so I have to head back home. I'm really sorry."

He let out a silent sigh, crestfallen. "Okay," he said. "Some other time, maybe."

"Yeah, sure."

He hesitated for a moment, and tried again, because what the fuck. "But since you're already in my car, can I at least give you a ride home?"

Demi's soft pink lips curved. She barely hesitated. "That would be great."

The Monster coughed, burped and died at that moment. He started it up again, embarrassed. His creaky old Frankencar was made of salvaged parts from defunct vehicles. Only his considerable skill at keeping engines alive kept her running, but aesthetically, the Monster was a zombie nightmare, with most of her upholstery rotted away. "Keep your leg away from the car door," he advised. "If that old exposed glue gets stuck to your jeans, it won't ever come off."

She angled her shapely leg away from the door. "Don't worry about it."

He drove for a few blocks, racking his brains for an opening. He wanted badly to ask if Boyd made a habit of bothering her, but that seemed too possessive a topic to open with right off the bat. So he went with the next random thing that popped into his head.

"I'm sorry you disappeared at lunchtime," he said. "I was going to ask you out for a drink then, but I missed my chance."

Demi snorted. "Raelene got a bee in her bonnet about having me do inventory."

"Bet that urgency went away once I left, am I right?" He turned onto the street that would take them onto Lakeshore Drive, a more leisurely and roundabout way to get over to Osborn Grade, the road that led up to the Heights. Demi didn't object.

So far, so good.

She slanted him a sly look through her dark, curling eyelashes. "Are you one of those guys who thinks that every single thing is about them?"

He laughed. "No, I am not one of those guys."

"Good," she murmured. Her smile was mysterious. "I'm sorry I'm busy tonight."

Exultation bubbled up inside him. "I didn't have a lot of time to spend anyhow," he said. "I have to be at my next job at eight o'clock. But I didn't want to wait."

"Another job? Where?"

He slowed to a crawl on Lakeshore Drive, brazenly pushing his luck. "I'm the night janitor up at the Fair Oaks Care Home," he explained.

"All day at a construction site, and then a night shift? Yikes. When do you sleep?"

"I don't," he admitted. "Not much, anyway. I get a couple hours from four to six AM. And I try to nap for a few minutes in between shifts down in the park by the Falls."

"That sounds nice, if it wasn't for the mosquitoes," she said.

"They don't bother me," he said. "Then I have a weekend shift at the gas station up on the highway. I'm saving up money to go into business for myself."

"Really? What business?"

"I'm designing an efficiency app," he told her. "To help streamline workflow in big organizations, like the military. I got the idea on my first combat tour, and I've been working on developing it ever since."

"You mean, on your own? Did you study computer science someplace?"

"Not formally," he admitted. "Self-taught."

Her eyebrows shot up. "No shit? You can self-teach that kind of stuff?"

"Sure. I couldn't afford college, and I was already enlisted in the Marines at that point, so I just downloaded course materials from MIT and Stanford's computer science classes and used my free time to do the course work. I watched the video lectures, did all the reading and the projects, took the exams. The info's all online. So I don't have any degree to show for it, but I have all the skills."

She stared at him. "Huh. You must be really mentally organized. To do it alone."

"I guess so," he said. "That got pounded into me real early, along with a shitload of math. And it's easy to learn when you're motivated."

"But doesn't it cost a lot to develop an app? Don't you need investors?"

"It's less expensive if you do most of the work yourself," he explained. "I've already sketched it out with wire-framing tools, and I'm researching the tech stacking and the programming languages. Right now I'm designing a custom back-end so it can grow and scale. And I'm working on the code. At least I was before I took on the janitorial job."

"Crazy," she said. "Who knew you were secretly an egghead computer nerd."

He felt suddenly embarrassed. Babbling like an idiot, trying to impress her. "I'm hung up on the visual design, though," he admitted. "I'm no artist, so I'll have to scrape up some cash and pay someone to help me make it all look good. But the more of the basic code I can write myself, the less expensive it'll ultimately be."

"That's incredible," she said. "Yay, you. I hope it goes well."

"Me, too. What about you? What are you doing back here in Shaw's Crossing? I figured you'd be working in the family business. In Granger Valley, or Tacoma."

She made a face. "So do my parents, my grandad and absolutely everyone else in this town. They think I'm destined to take over Shaw's Paper Products. That I'm the scion of stationery supplies. The crown princess of packing materials. But it's not my jam. To my family's eternal dismay."

"Ah," he said. "So what is?"

"Cooking." The announcement sounded almost defiant. "I want to be a professional chef."

He was startled, but he made the adjustment fast. "Of course. Those sandwiches you make are kick-ass."

She let out a crack of wry laughter. "Don't judge my skills on the basis of my lunch sandwiches."

"Why not? They're excellent."

"That's very sweet of you. But yes, that is my dream. I got a degree in restaurant management in college. In a few weeks, I start an internship at a restaurant in Seattle, and after that's done, I'm headed to the Culinary Institute. Some people get all excited in stationery stores, and I wish that was me, but I get worked up when I see a lump of goat cheese rolled in fresh cut herbs or cracked black pepper. Or lemon infused olive oil, or a really good pickled artichoke. What can you do? That's just what I'm made of."

No more delaying the inevitable. Eric turned onto Cedar Crest Drive, Demi's street, but he stopped well short of the driveway leading up to the huge Victorian mansion with the vast rolling lawn.

Their mailbox was knocked partly over, tilted at a forty-five degree angle to the ground. "What's with your mailbox?" he asked.

"Oh, that." Demi rolled her eyes. "That's Burt's work. Burt Colby. We have a problematic neighbor who sometimes drives himself home from the bar at two in the morning after a few too many beers. No one's gotten around to fixing it yet."

He grunted in disapproval. "That's dangerous. He could hurt someone."

"Yeah, he could, but he hasn't yet, other than our mailbox. Thanks for the ride, and for the nice comments about my sandwiches. Good luck with your app. It sounds awesome. I'm sure you'll be very successful."

Her incandescent smile struck him speechless. Lush pink lips, the perfect curve of her cheek. That sexy flush lighting up the tanned, perfect glow of her skin.

The window rattled dangerously in the door as Demi opened it. She hesitated, leaned over and kissed him on the cheek. Just a soft, glancing touch, but oh God. *Wow.*

"Have a good shift at the care home," she said. "Hope you get some sleep. See you tomorrow, maybe? At lunch?"

"Oh, yeah," he said, dazed. "I'll be there."

Sleep, hah. Like he was ever going to sleep again, with that rush of *gimme gimme* hormone pumping into his body. Damn right, she'd see him tomorrow. And the day after, and the day after that. And any chance he got, until he felt those lips against his skin again.

The place she'd kissed tingled wildly. Hyper-sensitized. Like it was glowing.

"Shall we get that milkshake you offered me after work tomorrow?" she asked.

"I'd love to, but this is the thing. I'll be all hot and sweaty, and my janitorial shift is at eight. I need to clean up before I put on the uniform. Usually I go straight to Kettle River Park and take a dip at Circle Falls. I keep a fresh uniform in the car to put on after."

She bit her lip as she thought it through. "I like swimming," she said. "And I like Circle Falls. Let's just go straight there. I'll bring a swimsuit to work."

"Yeah?" Exultation threatened to float him right up out of his seat. "You're on."

"I'll meet you outside the Bakery Café. Five o'clock."

"Great. Can I get your phone number?"

She was pulling out her phone, opening her mouth to reply when the sharp squeak of car tires coming to an abrupt halt focused his eyes beyond Demi's face, over her shoulder and to the other car.

Elaine Vaughn's horrified eyes, through the window of her BMW. Demi's mom.

Crap timing, but he regretted nothing.

Demi looked around. "Oh, shit," she whispered. "I gotta go."

"Sorry if I made problems for you," he called after her.

"Not at all. I'm just late getting dinner started, that's all.

See you around."

"Yeah. See you."

Demi cut in front of her mom's car as she crossed the street and headed up and across the huge lawn, straight toward the house.

Elaine Vaughan just sat as if she'd been turned into a statue. Eric looked patiently back at her, resisting the impulse to lay on the gas and escape, as if he were some lurking thug who'd done something wrong. He fucking wasn't. So he just sat there.

Besides, it felt vaguely disrespectful to drive off before she did. Like hanging up on someone.

Mrs. Vaughan finally turned straight ahead, tight-lipped. Her car surged ahead.

Well, fuck. He'd definitively ruined Demi's evening. Smooth move, bonehead.

He'd been trying so hard to walk the line. Head down, eyes forward, pocketing every spare penny to put toward his app. Then Demi Vaughan came into his line of vision, with her glossy brown curls and her hip-swaying walk, and whammo. His better judgment got coshed on the head, tied up and stuffed into the trunk of a car.

This was such a dumb move. On so many levels. He was the Prophet's spawn, she was a rich girl, the town princess, the college grad. He was practically broke, she lived in the biggest house in Shaw's Crossing. He was an orphan with a past best not talked about, and she was the granddaughter of the guy whose family gave the town its very name.

That was the girl he got a raging hard-on for. Because evidently he liked to punch up the challenge. Keep it interesting for himself. True to form.

He kept seeing the scene tomorrow, at the river, in his mind's eye. Demi soaking wet. Clingy, scanty clothes. Her cloud of dark hair floating around her. Nipples tight from the cold.

He hit the accelerator. The sudden burst of speed knocked the wobbling window right off its track, and it fell down inside the car door with a loud, decisive *thunk.*

Aw, shit.

He could still hear his better judgment back there, trapped in the trunk. Howling, kicking out the taillights, trying to be heard. But he just couldn't listen to it.

*Stay down, you noisy dickwad. I got things to do.*

# 3

"Demi? Honey? What on earth did I see out there?"

Her mother's shrill tone made Demi's mouth tighten as she rubbed the chicken with seasoned salt.

"Nothing, Mom," she said evenly. "Don't know what you're talking about."

"You were right on the street! Anyone could have seen you with him! Your father could have looked out the window and…and—"

"Seen me sitting in a guy's car? Oh, please." Demi packed the chunks of sliced celery, onion and potato around the chicken in the pan. "Come on, Mom."

"Don't you get flip with me, young lady!"

"What's this about?" Dad appeared in the kitchen entryway. Both of them glanced down at the ice cubes rattling in the glass of Scotch he held. Dad shifted until the hand holding the glass was out of sight behind the door frame. "What's going on?"

Her mother's lips were compressed. "She was sitting in

a parked car out on the street right in front of our house," she said. "With Eric Trask."

Her father's face went blank. "You're joking."

"Oh, stop it. Both of you," Demi said impatiently. "I wasn't making out with him. Not that it would have made any difference if I had been."

"Shut up," her father said. "And go to your room."

Demi stared at him, startled at his tone. Then she looked down at her greasy, salty hands. "Excuse me?" she said. "Dad, come on. I'm fixing dinner, and I—"

"Get out of this room. I don't want to look at you."

The tone of his voice was chilling. It sounded almost like…hatred.

Demi went to the sink and washed her hands with dish soap in the deathly silence that followed. She washed them carefully, taking her time. Then she dried them the same way. Slow. Methodical. She was an adult. She did not scurry. She had her dignity.

By the time she marched past her father, righteous anger had replaced her shock.

"Maybe you two haven't made the adjustment yet, but I'm no longer a child to be sent to my room," she told him. "I'm an adult. I have been for a while. Get used to it."

"Get out of my sight," Dad repeated.

She tried not to flinch. "I'd be glad to. Permanently, if necessary."

When she got to her room, Demi's knees gave way. She thudded down on her bed.

Her legs shook. She'd been in conflict with Dad for more or less her entire life, but this level of hostility from him was new. And shocking.

She wouldn't have expected Dad to be happy about her

spending time with Eric Trask, after all the trash talk that had been thrown around about the guy. But this furious venom was, well…out of proportion was an understatement.

She wondered if her father was afraid of the Prophet's Curse, like Raelene. Maybe he, too, had subconsciously pinned that big death cluster that happened eight years ago on Eric and his brothers. There was no one else left to pin it on, after all. Not after the fire.

But what the hell? That was sloppy thinking. Childish and superstitious and unfair. She expected better out of these people. Even Dad, in spite of his many shortcomings.

She wished she could pack up her stuff and stomp out in a huff, but as usual, it was never that simple. Her ex-college roommate, Rory, was working in Seattle. Rory had offered to let Demi couch-surf for the duration of her internship. But Rory was on a business trip on the east coast right now, and Demi couldn't afford to blow her limited savings on a hotel room in a big, expensive city just out of pique.

No, she would be sensible. Keep her head down. Wait for Rory to get back. Plus, she was still hoping for a loan from Granddad to help with the tuition at the Culinary Institute, since Mom and Dad had refused to help. Just on principle.

And damn it, she wanted to see Eric again. She was an adult, for fuck's sake. It wasn't like she wanted to marry the guy. She was leaving Shaw's Crossing. She had no intention of coming back, other than a holiday duty visit now and then.

So maybe she would indulge in some fun with him, if the opportunity presented itself. Discreetly, and with all due precautions. It was her own damn business, after all. No one else on earth needed to know.

Maybe Dad would toss her out on the street if he found out. So be it. She'd figure out something on the fly. She was too old to be shoved around and dictated to.

This was no big deal. Just a hormonal buzz, for the entertainment value. A little light flirtation to make the hot summer days pass faster.

Where was the harm in that?

# 4

After long deliberation, Demi had decided that the matching purple sports bra and boy shorts could pass as a sporty bathing suit if you squinted. It was good enough for a quick dip in Kettle River Park, so no need to change after work. She got through her shift somehow in a fever of excitement.

At five, she washed up in the staff bathroom, wishing she could primp, but she was about to jump into a river, so just a little water-proof mascara, a slick of lip gloss and a few quick strokes of her brush would have to do.

She came out to find Raelene out on the sidewalk, leaning to lecture Eric through the open window of his car. "…cannot park here! This is right in front of my business!"

"It's okay, Raelene," Demi told her. "We were just leaving."

She got in, waving at Raelene's disapproving face, and rocked back against the seat as the car accelerated. In the broken rearview mirror, two different angles of Raelene frowned after her, hands on her hips.

"The getaway car," she said. "Punch it. Feels so good."

"Hard day?" Eric asked.

He was so sweatily gorgeous, she immediately lost her train of thought when she looked at him. "Uh, yes," she admitted, angling her knee away from the exposed upholstery glue. "Might be my last day. Raelene and I have had some pretty stark differences of opinion lately."

Eric took the lakefront road that headed out to Kettle River Park. "I'm sorry. I should have picked you up somewhere else."

"No." Her voice was forceful. "I won't tolerate being pushed around anymore. Not from Raelene, or my folks, or my granddad."

"Shit." Eric pounded the steering wheel. "I didn't want to make trouble for you."

"Don't worry. I can manage. And I've been looking forward to a dip into Circle Falls since you mentioned it yesterday, so let's go for it."

His teeth flashed in a boyish grin. "Actually, I know an even better place that's just a little further upriver."

"Great. Lead on."

Demi was glad she'd worn her rugged sports sandals as they hiked through the park down to the riverbed and up toward the big crescent-shaped shelf of rock in the canyon with water thundering over it into the big pool below. Several people were swimming there, but they didn't stop. She followed Eric up the hill along the river on a narrow, pebbled path through the tumbled boulders, along a mossy cliff face and through a jumble of huge, tumbled tree trunks. Once through that barrier, they crept alongside the stream for a while under a long, dim overhang of rock. Eric was so tall, he had to bend double. Tufts of moss dripped water onto her neck.

Out into the sunshine again, and Eric led her back up the side of the canyon and out onto a big outcropping of rock.

From there, Demi looked down at a deep pool of rippling, churning water that glowed a beautiful, deep green-blue. Dragonflies glimmered in a darting blue cloud at the calmer edge. Not a soul was in sight. The water was deep and clear.

"I've never been this far above the falls." Her voice cut off into a gasp as Eric stripped off his shirt.

Whew. It ought to be illegal. So big, but not beefcake big. Just lots of thick, lean, sinewy muscle. A workman's tan, blistered from previous sunburns. Darker on his neck and arms. Faint, silvery scars on his back moved, snakelike, as he stretched and flexed.

He hesitated before shucking his jeans, glancing over his shoulders. "You don't mind seeing me in my underwear, do you?"

"Not if you don't mind seeing mine," she said.

His grin dazzled her. "I hope I can handle it." The jeans dropped.

It was no surprise that his legs were as fine as the rest of him. She didn't get a very long look, just one glimpse of his stunning ass, taut and muscular.

He flew off the rocks in a perfect, knife-like dive and came up splashing and laughing, his gorgeous white teeth and dimples on full display.

"Cold?" she asked, stepping out of her cut-offs.

His eyes never left her body. "Nah. It's balmy. Tropical."

"Bullshitter." She wrenched off her T-shirt. "I know this river as well as you do. Even in July it's freaking cold."

His smile faded as he stared intently at her body in the jogging bra and boy shirts. She started to blush. Only one cure for that.

She launched herself off the rock and hit the water. Oh. So. *Cold.*

She came up for air and flung her hair back, gasping as the current grabbed her. It jerked her along, faster and harder than she could fight it. She put all her muscle into it, struggling against the pull to get to the side of the river—

And smacked up right against Eric's huge, wet bare chest. His arms wound around her and held her steady as the water churned and pounded against her back.

"Fuck, I'm sorry," he gasped out, dashing water from his eyes. "What a goddamn idiot I am. I forgot that the current would be different for you. You're so much smaller."

She put her hands against his shoulders. "I'm fine. I wasn't in any danger, I don't think. We just would've had to meet up somewhere downstream, that's all. No biggie."

"I should never have let that happen."

"Oh, stop it. I'm fine. It was wild. Exciting. I loved it."

The energy shifted as they stared at each other. "You like wild?" he asked.

Demi pushed her clinging hair back off her forehead. "Yes."

"Is that why you're here with me?"

The tension in his tone made her cautious. "I'm not sure exactly what you mean."

His big shoulders lifted and then dropped. "You know. Walking on the wild side. Slumming with the animal that escaped from the zoo."

Her mouth dropped open for a moment before she found her voice. "Screw you."

Eric looked started. "Hey. I didn't mean to—"

"I don't care what you meant or didn't mean. You're being dickish and defensive about something that has nothing to do with me."

His brow knit into a frown. "I didn't mean to do that."

"I'm here because I like you, Eric. At least, I did. But if you're going to feel sorry for yourself and blame me for someone else's bullshit, then count me out." She shoved him, breaking his grip, and flung herself into the current's muscular pull once again.

Eric leaped in after her. After a few moments of being swooped and tossed in the center of the current, he got her back to the side of the river again, trapping her between himself and a sheer, towering expanse of rock.

He held her there, immobile. Water swirled and churned around them. "I'm sorry, okay?" he said. "I've gotten that before. Girls who want to feel wild, piss off their parents, make their boyfriends jealous. I just wondered if that was what was going on here."

She shoved at his chest, but couldn't break his grip this time. "It appears that nothing is going on here," she said. "Let go of me. Right now."

"In this current? That's nuts. I can't. It's not safe."

"I don't need safe. And I don't need to walk on the wild side, either," she said. "I can find my way to the wild side all by myself. I am dangerous as all shit. With no help from you. I do not need to live anything vicariously through you. Got it?"

"Loud and clear."

They just studied each other fiercely, as if trying to see inside the other's head.

"You said you're here because you like me," he said.

"Liked," she snapped. "Liked is the operative word."

"Ah." He considered that for a moment. "What if I said I was sorry again? Would you like me again?"

"Depends," she said. "Some guys apologize better than others."

"What if I apologized like this?" He yanked her closer.

He covered her mouth with his, and Demi had just a moment of disorientation, an instant of *who-the-fuck-does-this-guy-think-he-is*, her hands up against his chest to shove him away…and then she felt it.

A flash, blazing through her. A rush of wild energy uncoiling in her body. Heat. Light, bursting behind her eyes. A throb of startled yearning way down low.

She was motionless, astonished. Feeling it take her, fill her. His lips were so soft. It was cold in that water, but not the sweet heat of his mouth.

So hot. Oh God.

Heat flared in her mouth, her chest, her belly, between her legs. Flowering and spreading everywhere. She pulled back, gasping for air. The swirl of water sucked hard at her legs. Eric was as steady as an oak.

He kept her close, legs apart, braced around hers. "You're not the only one who likes it wild," he murmured into her ear.

They stared at each other, and by some mutual, wordless accord, their lips came together again. Tasting each other tenderly, exploring the sweetness, the smoothness, the heat, the shapes of each other's lips. His tongue, touching, twining.

Her fingers dug into his chest, making him growl with satisfaction and kiss her more hungrily. Her arms wound around his neck. She struggled to free her legs from between his clamped thighs so she could wrap them round his waist.

He helped her, cupping her ass to hold her up against himself. The kiss got hotter, harder, wilder. It felt frantic, almost like anger.

The power flooding her was a revelation. It was magic. It made her feel superhuman. It rose up from deep within like a column of heat and light, unstoppable.

She forgot who she was. Problems, past, future, ambitions, plots and plans, they all dissolved into sensation. She just sought more of his hot, marauding mouth, his tough, sinewy body holding her. Handling her with masterful authority.

His kiss called forth a depth of feeling that she'd never felt, but she gave it to him. Helplessly, eagerly. She wound around his body, ready right now for anything he wanted. Practically whimpering with eagerness to have him inside of her.

He lifted his mouth from hers and started to move, shifting them into a more sheltered, hidden crack between two enormous rocks. They were still chest deep, and she was intensely conscious of the thick, hot bulge of his erect penis prodding her belly.

She moved against it eagerly, and he groaned deep in his throat. Their eyes locked as she leaned back for air. His eyes were so beautiful. Bright silver gray, banded with dark slate. Brilliant with raw, pure hunger.

Her throat was locked with excitement, but he closed his eyes, hissing out a sharp breath. "We can't," he said, hoarsely. "No latex."

Reality flickered fitfully in her mind. Context. Consequences. Latex. Of course. Thank God someone was being a grown-up. But she wanted to scream in frustration.

Eric kissed her again, holding her against himself with

one hand but slipping his other hand down over her belly to her mound, petting her through the wet fabric of her boy shorts. The contact made her shiver and convulse in his arms. She moved against his hand. Couldn't stop moving. Grabbed his arm, pulling it closer. Pushing his hand deeper.

He slid his hand beneath her waistband and slipped it inside, sliding lower. Teasing her clit, rolling it tenderly against his thumb. Petting her pussy lips, oh so delicately. Opening them. Spreading her hot slickness around. Very slowly, penetrating her. They moaned together, shivering, as he pushed his finger inside, still stroking her clit.

"Oh God, Demi," he said, his voice rough. "Smooth as silk. Your pussy is so hot."

She was beyond any coherent response. She was gasping and whimpering at his slow, perfect caresses. He worked her clit expertly as his finger thrust inside.

She clenched around him and cried out as the sensations crested. Huge, deep throbs of delight pumped rhythmically through every part of her body.

After, she floated in his arms, limp and shivering. She'd never felt anything like that in any of her adventures with her college or high school boyfriends. Some of which had been fun. Some of which had been meh. None of them had moved her like this.

The towering hugeness of this feeling—it was dangerous. It could shatter her. Send her flying out into space in a thousand jagged pieces.

She lifted her hot face from his shoulder. His beautiful eyes were somber. He waited patiently. His stiff penis poked up out of his underwear, long and thick and blunt.

She reached into his briefs and gripped him. That was a lot of man. Stiff, rock hard. His heartbeat throbbing in her hands. She touched him, first one hand, then the other, sliding, squeezing. Then both together.

He gasped, gripping her stroking hands. Tightening her clasp and guiding her into moving faster, rougher than she would have on her own. He went rigid, head thrown back.

"Oh. Fuck. Me," he choked out.

She felt the jerking pulses of his orgasm against her trapped hands.

They swayed together in the water, wordless, for several minutes. Speechless.

Eric was the first to raise his head. "I want to go down on you so bad," he told her. "I could lick your pussy for hours. Make you come, over and over. Until you're exhausted from it. I want to taste you but the water washes all your lube away."

Demi tried to speak, but had to clear her throat. "I would return the favor."

"Oh man," he groaned. "Torture."

"Agony," she agreed.

He buried his face in her wet hair, taking her earlobe between his teeth. Delicately biting, then sucking on it, making her shiver and dig her fingernails deeper into his shoulders.

"This is fucking killing me," he said. "But I have to get back to town now if I want to get to the care home on time for my shift. God, it's hard."

"I understand," she said. "Just as well. Considering."

"I guess." He nuzzled her neck, nibbling it delicately. "After my shift tomorrow, I have a free evening. My only one all week. No night shift at the care home until day after tomorrow."

Excitement curled her toes, which were still twined

around his legs, braced against his calves. "Oh, really? And?"

"Do you like waterfalls?"

She laughed. "Duh! Isn't it obvious?"

He grinned. "I know a place," he said. "A special place. I'd like to show it to you."

"Tell me," she said. "I'm intrigued."

"It's hard to get to, though. Are you afraid of heights?"

"Not unreasonably so," she told him. "But I'm no free climber."

"There's no free climbing involved, but it's steep, and there's some rock scrambling and narrow cliff trails. Only if you're up to it. It's not in any book or trail map. And the fact that it's hard to get to is what makes it special." He paused. "And private."

Fresh excitement made her fingers tighten on his upper arms. "How do you know about it?"

"Found it when I was a kid, with my brothers. No one would bother us there."

The velvety, caressing tone in her voice was intensely seductive. She imagined the two of them somewhere private, no one to bother them. Wildly sensual images filled her mind, making her heart race. "Sounds…nice."

"It will be," he assured her. "I'll make damn sure of it. Are we on?"

"Yes," she said.

His face lit up, and something inside her combusted at the sight. "Excellent," he said. "Put your legs around me again. I'll walk you back to where we left our clothes."

Demi laughed. "Sounds dangerous. Putting my legs around you, I mean."

"You know me," he muttered into her ear. "I like dangerous."

It took a long time to get back to the rocks where they had left their clothes. Not so much because of the strength of the current. Eric was immensely strong. The delay was because he kept stopping in mid-current to kiss her.

They were in a terrible state of mindless, shuddering lust by the time he pulled her into the calmer water of the pool they'd leaped into. Teetering on the verge of forgetting caution and consequences.

The laughter from above them brought them to their senses. Kids were clambering on the sides of the canyon, hooting and catcalling down at them. Teenagers. No one she knew, but there they were, watching and snickering and shouting off-color jibes.

Eric set her down, trying to tuck himself into his briefs. That was a lost cause. No underwear could contain a hard-on like that. They clambered up onto the rocks, and Eric pulled a smallish, threadbare towel out of his bag, offering it to her.

She shook her head. "You're the one who has to make yourself presentable for work," she said. "I can change when I get home."

More giggling and hooting above prompted Eric to wrap the towel around his waist. He changed under it, pulling on the fresh clothes from his bag while she pulled her own over her wet underwear.

They looked at each other in a spasm of mutual shyness, then both laughed.

"Meet you after work again tomorrow?" he asked. "Same time?"

She nodded.

He reached out to take her hand. "I'll park in front of the bookstore this time. So I don't get Raelene all bent out of shape."

Demi floated the whole way back, even while rock scrambling. Her body felt as light as a cloud and full of feverish energy. Bounding from stone to stone, springy and bold and sure-footed, never missing a step.

Back in the park, people noticed their clasped hands. Heads turned, but they couldn't be bothered to take note of who was looking. They didn't talk much, but the energy from his hand rushed up her arm and then filled her completely, charging her with giddy excitement. She was sorry when they reached his car.

Eric opened her door for her and then got into the driver's side. "Remember to watch out for that upholstery glue," he reminded her. "This car doesn't usually carry passengers, so it doesn't have company manners."

"I'm fine with it," she assured him.

"I call it the Monster," he told her. "My Frankencar. I stitched it together out of a bunch of dead cars and raised it from the dead with unholy magic, so it's got some foul zombie spooge oozing out in a few places. Or is that too much information?"

She laughed. "I think it's awesome that you have the power to raise zombie cars from the dead. Is that an actual superpower, or just a side hobby for you?"

"More like a necessity," he said. "I look forward to the day that I can buy a car that's not a relic from a bygone age. Even just something that was manufactured during my own lifetime would be great."

"Did you learn how to do that from Otis?"

"Nah, I picked that up when I was younger, up at GodsAcre," Eric said. "Old Jeremiah had this thing about the apocalypse being right around the corner, so we needed to be ready to make machines run again after the big electromagnetic pulse wiped out the power grid and gutted civilization as we know it. So he favored really old cars. The ones made before they started putting computers in everything. That's my Monster. Made to roam the blasted wasteland after the Great Fall, scavenging for food scraps and fuel."

Demi gave him a sidewise look, not quite sure what response was appropriate after an admission like that. "Wow," she said quietly. "Dark."

"Yeah, that's Jeremiah for you," Eric said. "He was all kinds of dark."

"Did you believe it? At the time, I mean?"

Eric hesitated for a long moment. "I guess I did," he admitted. "I was living inside that reality, and I didn't have anything else to compare it to. And Jeremiah was extremely convincing. Besides, the way things are going, it could still end up just like he said."

"It could, at that," she agreed. "It must have been so strange for you and your brothers afterwards. The outside world. I mean, above and beyond the fire."

"We didn't notice much of anything for a while." Eric kept his eyes straight ahead. "Our world was gone. Such as it was. It was messed up, yes, but it was all we knew."

"It was just the three of you who survived?"

"Four, if you count Fiona. We smuggled her out about a week before."

That pricked her ears up. "Who was Fiona? Smuggled? How?"

"She was another GodsAcre kid," he said. "At the end, right before the fire, the whole place had gone crazy. Fiona was only fifteen, but Jeremiah gave permission to this slimeball pedophile Kimball to marry her. He was twenty-five years older than her. She tried to run away, and she got dragged back and publicly flogged. It pissed us all off, but Anton went totally batshit. I suspect he had a thing for her, though he'd never admit it."

"That's terrible," she whispered.

"We busted her out right before her wedding day. Or to be precise, Anton busted her out. Mace and I just did as we were told. Stole money from the treasury, got her a bus ticket to her aunt in California. Mace and I covered for them while Anton and Fiona hiked cross country down to town. He got her to the station and onto the bus. So yeah, Fiona definitely counts as a GodsAcre survivor. Which makes four of us."

Demi blew out a slow, shaky sigh. "That's an incredible story," she said. "I never heard about her."

"Yeah, I guess nobody did," Eric admitted. "Why would they? The three of us were the only ones alive who knew about her, and we didn't tell anyone. She was well away from it all, and we were glad for her. We didn't want her to have to talk to the cops and the journalists and all the rest. God, what a fucking zoo that all was."

"Did you guys get into trouble at GodsAcre? For helping her escape, I mean?"

Eric was silent for an unnerving interval. "Yes," he said.

His tone made her stomach go heavy with dread. "Oh, no," she murmured. "I'm sorry. Never mind, Eric. Don't tell me if I'm intruding—"

"Kimball flogged all of us for what we did," Eric said. "But he turned Anton's back into hamburger. He almost killed him. Jeremiah didn't even try to stop him."

"Oh God, Eric. I'm so sorry."

"Didn't mean to be a downer." His voice was grim.

"But if you start poking around in my past, you'll turn up some bad shit. There's a lot of it."

"I didn't mean to pry," she said. "I wish I hadn't asked."

"I don't mind you knowing," he said. "But I'm trying to move forward. That's all in the past. Dead and gone. It can't hurt me now."

"What about your brothers? Are they doing the same thing? Moving on, I mean?"

"Yeah, they're okay. Mace is crushing it in the Marines. Force Recon. He loves it in the military, way more than I did. Anton is actually turning into a sort of celebrity in Las Vegas. He's a DJ now, mixing tracks, producing albums. Doing the rounds of the big dance clubs. People go nuts for his stuff."

"I can just imagine what Otis thinks of that, knowing him," Demi said.

"Yeah, you got it. Otis understands the military, but Anton's DJ gig, and my tech project, that stuff leaves him bewildered. It seems frivolous and decadent to him. He and Jeremiah would have been in perfect agreement on that score, though I'd never say that to Otis's face. It would bug the shit out of him."

He parked farther from her house than last time. The porch lights blazed.

"Give me your number," he said. "I can't call or text you from Otis's, because there's no cell service out there. But I want your number for when I'm in town."

"Of course. Give me yours, too. I'll plug in my number, you plug in yours."

They entered the numbers, passed phones back and stared at each other, smiling. Reluctant to break the connection. It felt so good.

"I have to run," he said regretfully. "I want to kiss you again so bad, it hurts. But that would be pushing our luck. Besides, when I get going I just can't stop."

She reached out and grabbed his hand, squeezing it. "Thanks for telling me…you know. About your past," she said awkwardly. "So…tomorrow, then. 'Night."

It felt silly to just sit there holding his hand, but when she tugged it, he wouldn't let go. Suddenly that alchemy that had overcome her in the river rose up again like a wave of warm excitement, wafting her upwards. She didn't even need the catalyst of a kiss to get the reaction going. Her feverish memory filled in the blanks. Every detail of those wild, breathless kisses. The pounding water, his massive chest, the quick strong throb of his heart when she gripped his cock, squeezing and stroking the long, stiff, hot—

*Stop. This. Now.*

But Eric bent over her hand, pulling it up to his lips and began to kiss it.

The slow, wonderfully deliberate touch of his lips to her skin stirred her deeply. Everything connected to everything, and all of it was excited by him. Shivers ran along the surface of her skin. Delicious mini-orgasms. A growing, keening ache of anticipation.

After a few minutes of getting her hand kissed she was red and shaking, about to come right there. Her body shimmered with intense awareness.

"Eric," she whispered.

He kissed her knuckles one by one. So tenderly. "Yeah?"

"You're pushing our luck. Big time."

"Maybe," he said. "I want to push it into a whole new dimension." He moved on to her fingertips, suckling them tenderly.

"You'll be late to your shift." Her voice was quivering.

Eric sighed sharply and pressed her fingers against his cheek. Hot, and velvety. Strong, jutting bones. The scratchy rasp of new beard. "Tomorrow, then," he said.

"Yes," she whispered. "Tomorrow."

And still she sat there. Unable to move.

"If you stay in this car, I'm going to start ravishing your hands again." There was a hint of laughter in his voice.

That finally got her out of the car. Eric just sat there, resting his elbow on the open window, making no move to go. "I can't leave here until you're safely inside," he told her.

Aw. How gallant and old-fashioned. She was so charmed, it took all the willpower she had to turn her back on his outrageously gorgeous smile and walk away.

Feeling intensely observed with every step.

Mom and Dad were waiting for her in the dining room. Her giddy high subsided as soon as she saw their faces. Both had that tense, puckered look that she had come to dread. Granddad Shaw, her mom's father, was also there, but to his credit, he didn't have the disapproval pucker on his seamed face. He just looked worried.

"Finally." Dad's voice was heavy and cold. "You're home."

Demi glanced at the antique clock on the mantelpiece. "It's only five minutes to eight."

"Where were you?" her mother asked.

"I was hot, after a shift at the Bakery Café," she said. "I went down to the park and took a dip at Circle Falls."

"With Eric Trask," her father said, eyeing her clinging T-shirt with distaste.

She forced herself to count down slowly from ten,

adjusting her tone before answering. "I don't want to be rude or disrespectful, but that's none of your business."

"Raelene called," her mother said. "She told me you'd gone off with that boy."

"He's a man, Mom. Twenty-four years old. He's not a criminal. He works really hard. Holds down three jobs. He barely sleeps. He's launching his own business."

Her father let out a derisive snort. "Hah. I'd like to see that happen."

"So would I," Demi said. "It would be great, and he deserves a break. What is it with you guys? What do you have against him?"

Her father slammed down his hand on the table. "He's dangerous!" he roared. "He was brought up in a madhouse—"

"That's not his fault!"

"It doesn't matter," her mother said earnestly. "Honey, listen. Just because it's not his fault doesn't make it not true, or not dangerous. Damage is damage. I hate to say it, because Otis is our friend, and it was generous and brave of him to take them in. But those boys are ticking bombs just waiting to go off. Sooner or later it'll happen, and I don't want you anywhere near him when it does."

"Eric is not a ticking bomb. You are all prejudiced against him, for no good reason. I expected better of you. He's hard working and ambitious, and I respect that."

"Honey, please. It's not just the boy," Mom hurried on. "He's just a symptom of a much larger problem. These hazardous choices. They could put a big dent in your future."

"You mean changing my major, the Culinary Institute, the internship? Which things? What choices?"

"Watch your tone, young lady," her father said.

"The thing is, you just don't have the life perspective yet to understand the long-term consequences of the decisions you're making. You're the one who can take Shaw Paper Products into the new century. You just can't see it yet. So your grandfather has been talking it over with us, and we have decided together that we can't in all good conscience invest money in this…this fleeting whim of yours."

Her throat tightened. "It's not a whim. I've wanted this for years. I've worked part-time catering gigs since high school. This internship is an incredible opportunity for me."

"I know it looks that way to you, but it's just another bright shiny thing, honey."

"So what I'm hearing is, I'm on my own, for the tuition for the Culinary Institute," Demi said. "Just to be clear."

"Demi, honey, please. It doesn't make sense for us to throw away money on—"

"It's okay, Mom," she broke in. "I'll work it out on my own. If Eric can work three jobs to invest in his future, so can I."

"Honey, don't storm off!"

Demi stopped halfway up the stairs. "I'm not storming. Truly. I'm sorry you're so disappointed in my choices, but my mind's made up. Excuse me, please. I want to put on some dry clothes."

"Don't throw that attitude around when you're misbehaving!" her father roared.

Demi turned to face him. Her face was getting hotter. "Me, misbehaving?" she said slowly. "You're a fine one to talk about misbehaving."

"What the hell do you mean by that?"

"I know what happened at the Tacoma Distribution Center a few years ago, Dad. It was my senior year in high school. I was living here, remember? I overheard the yelling and screaming. It was hard to miss."

Her mother's eyes widened. "Demi, don't. That has nothing to do with—"

"You stole money from Shaw Paper Products," Demi said.

"I did not steal money!" Dad bellowed. "It was a misunderstanding! And every last cent was replaced!"

"Sure it was, once they caught you."

"Demi! Please, stop!" Mom sounded like she was about to burst into tears.

Demi barged on, unmoved. "That's why they moved you to the Granger Valley Distribution Center. It's smaller, right? Not so much money moving through, less temptation, less exposure, less probability of getting into trouble again. Wasn't that your reasoning, Granddad?"

Granddad sat there, expressionless, with his arms crossed over his chest. He neither confirmed nor denied her words. He didn't have to.

Dad lunged forward and slapped her face. She rocked back against the banister.

"Ben!" her mother yelled. "Don't!"

"That's enough, Benedict," Granddad barked. "Never do that again!"

"Honey, are you okay?" Her mother shoved her dad out of her way and started up the stairs, but Demi flinched away from her and retreated up the steps, her hand pressed to her face. This wasn't the worse slap she'd ever gotten from Dad, but it was always nasty and humiliating. She just could never learn to keep her big mouth shut.

"I'm fine," she said. "I'm used to it. I can't even breathe without pissing him off."

"Maybe you should come stay with me for a while, honey," Granddad said.

Demi stifled a groan, touched though she was by the offer. Granddad was great, but he breathed down her neck just as hard, in his own benevolent, stone-heavy way.

"Thanks, Granddad. I just need some time in my room alone."

All three shouted after her, a chorus of noise as she hurried up the stairs. She ignored them, desperate to get a locked door between herself and every last one of them.

She slid down onto the floor on her butt when the door was finally closed, and rubbed the hot, stinging spot on her cheek.

She couldn't stay here any longer. Not even for a few more weeks, to save money. She wasn't going to the Culinary Institute this year anyhow. Not on her own dime.

Change of plans. She had to go to Seattle now. Scramble to find enough flexible catering work that would fit around the hours of the internship. After that ended, she'd find the highest paying job she could during the day and double up with catering gigs for nights and weekends. She'd find a group house to manage big city rent. Eat leftovers after catering gigs. Shop at thrift stores. Take the bus or walk everywhere.

She would save every penny toward her goals. Just like Eric did.

Damn, the guy was inspiring in all kinds of delicious ways.

She would have bought her bus ticket that very moment, but for the date with Eric. First things first. She had to have one more taste of that wafting-six-inches-off-the-ground high, that scorching, mind-melting lust. Those earth-shattering orgasms.

That was her shining prize. She was going to reach out and take it.

God knows she might as well, since she'd already paid the price.

# 5

Eric was careful coming down the stairs that morning, skipping the ones that creaked and snapped. When he'd gotten home before dawn, he'd seen a motorcycle and a rented Buick parked out behind Otis's pick-up. His brothers had arrived. Mace was on leave from the Marines, so Otis had bullied Anton into driving out from his luxury lair in Vegas so they could be all in one place. It hardly ever happened these days, and never in Shaw's Crossing. Otis complained that getting them back here was like pulling teeth.

It was a quarter to six, and he moved through the hallway at that careful, panther-like pace that left plenty of time for his eyes to slide over the pictures in the entrance hall. His adoptive father was an avid birdwatcher and amateur wildlife photographer, and Otis's tired old joke was that the three boys he'd taken in definitely qualified as wildlife. So among the woodpeckers and red-tailed hawks and bald eagles and elk were pictures of himself, Anton and Mace. Fixing cars. Sprawled on the porch. Diving into the river pools.

One picture held pride of place, three photos displayed

in a single frame: a shot from each of their three high school graduation ceremonies. Cap, gown, and all.

Otis took full credit for that achievement, as well he should.

Almost to the door. Careful, now. If he managed not to wake anyone—

"Well, well." Anton's voice, from the kitchen. "Look who's sneaking out at the crack of dawn without even saying hello."

Eric froze, and accepted the inevitable. He was busted.

He entered the kitchen, where Otis, Anton and Mace sat at the table, wide awake and fully dressed. They were drinking their coffee and staring at him with varying degrees of worry and disapproval.

"Up bright and early, hmm?" Otis leaned forward, his gnarled, arthritis-knobbed hands clasping a coffee mug, and scowled at Eric from beneath bushy, tufted white eyebrows. Otis was craggy, keen-eyed, hawk-nosed. He'd let a grizzled beard grow in as long as it wanted to grow since his retirement from the job as police chief. That and the old plaid flannel shirt flapping on his bony frame made him look just like the rawhide-tough, old-time mountain man that he truly was.

"Morning," Eric said guardedly, nodding to his brothers. "Good to see you guys."

"Is it?" Anton slouched back in the kitchen chair in a pose that looked lazy and indolent, but knowing Anton, was anything but.

"You cut your hair," Eric said. "What the fuck? Your pride and joy. Gone."

Anton's hand went up, finger-combing the thick, messy, chopped-off brush of dark hair, shaved closer on the sides. "Got sick of dealing with it," he said. "All that combing, having it clog the fucking drain, the girls always rolling over it in bed—"

"Hold it right there." Otis clucked his tongue. "I don't want to hear any sex stuff."

Anton's brief grin flashed. "Sorry," he murmured, tussling his top hair. The gesture made the thick muscles of his chest flex beneath his gray tee-shirt. Anton wore a tee-shirt in Otis's house out of respect, to cover some of his extensive tattoo art, of which Otis vociferously disapproved. But the tattoos drew attention away from the snarl of whip scars on Anton's back, which Eric suspected was his brother's main reason for getting them.

He might have known they'd catch his sorry ass. His brothers were early risers. Or rather, shitty sleepers. All the brothers were twitchy, restless, and more-or-less paranoid. Relentless training to be the vanguard of Jeremiah's army of the faithful had jacked up their stress chemicals chronically high. Which sucked for sleep.

"Gone so soon?" Mace said. "We just got here. Sit down. Have some coffee."

"Nope, gotta run," he said. "Early shift down at the construction site."

"At six AM?" Anton said. "Well, that would explain the incredibly long shower."

Mace approached, sniffing him. "How much cologne did you splash on yourself, anyhow? Woodsy, spicy, with just a hint of bergamot to drive the ladies wild." He gave Eric's face a playful slap. "Ooh, feel that close shave. Smooth as a baby's bottom."

Eric jerked away. "Cut it out, meathead. What the fuck is this about?"

"Language," Otis growled. "Bad language is for mindless idiots."

Mace rose, grabbing a coffee mug from the cupboard. He filled it from the pot, and put it down in front of the one empty chair. "Sit," he said flatly.

Eric's gaze focused on the shiny burn scars on Mace's huge hands and thick forearms. Mace's souvenir of the GodsAcre fire, right out there for the world to look at and wonder about.

Mace was the biggest of the brothers. Both he and Anton were six-three, but Mace had just kept on growing into a dense wall of muscle, stopping just shy of six-five. Otis had been forced to buy kitchen chairs with metal frames after they destroyed his old ones.

Mace's dirt-blond buzz cut was fresh and crisp, not like his own that was getting shaggy on top. His younger brother had bright gray eyes. His beard scruff glinted reddish gold on his square jaw.

Otis indicated the chair with a commanding air. "Sit," he said. "We need to talk about a phone call I got last night from my old friend, Benedict Shaw."

Eric's eyes closed with a hiss of dismay. "Oh fuck."

"Language," Mace chided. "Your mindless idiocy is showing. But I can't really blame you for it. I've seen Demi Vaughan, and she has got one sweet set of plump, pointy-tipped—"

"Shut up," Eric snarled.

"Mason!" Otis scolded. "Show some respect for the young lady."

"Oh believe me, I've got nothing but respect for a pair of tits like—ow!"

Anton smacked Mace in the back of the head, knocking

his face into the table, all without looking away from Eric's face. Cups rattled, and Mace cursed and squawked but Anton didn't appear to notice. He was too busy staring right into Eric's brain.

Anton's dark gaze had a strange, almost hypnotic quality. Since he was a kid, when he stared at a person, it was like he saw inside them and could just poke around in there, opening cupboards and drawers, turning over rocks, rifling through anything he pleased.

He saw things Eric didn't even know about himself. Then he churned it through some mysterious processor in his head, deducing things he had no business knowing.

Anton shook his head. He looked almost pitying. "Dude," he said. "You're done for. It's all over your face. You've drunk from the sacred well. Kiss your ass goodbye."

"Oh, God." Otis put his head in his hands. "Say it's not true. Damn idiot."

Eric could not say it wasn't true. He kept his eyes averted and his mouth shut.

Mace could always be counted on to break an uncomfortable silence. "Whoa! Look!" he crowed, holding up a box of condoms that he'd fished out of Eric's backpack. "Bad intentions? The seal's not broken yet, but it won't be long now! Here, I'll do the honors for you." He ripped open the box.

"Get your paws out of my shit." Eric jerked the box away from him and the string of condoms tumbled down onto Otis's coffee mug, slid off and came to rest on the table in all their glory.

Otis rubbed his forehead as if it pained him. "For the love of God," he said. "You said you wanted to work like a bastard and put aside some money for your future, and now you're diddling Henry Shaw's granddaughter? That's insane. That girl is off-limits."

"Her limits are her own to decide." Eric folded up the condoms and shoved them roughly back into the box. "She's not a child. It's not up to her dad, or granddad, or you, or anyone. And it's nobody's damn business what we do."

Otis muttered under his breath, shaking his head.

"Sorry. I have to go," Eric mumbled, slinging his bag over his shoulder.

"We'll discuss this when you get home," Otis said. "Tonight's your night off from the care home, right? You and your brothers can all help me clean out the storage shed."

"Uh…" Eric hesitated. "I'll be home late. I got something going on after."

Mace chuckled under his breath. "Oh, I just bet he'll get something going on. Something as juicy and sweet and silky soft like a ripe—"

"Shut up!" Otis and Eric yelled.

Eric locked eyes with Otis. Not blinking, since he had nothing to be ashamed of.

Otis shook his head wearily. "After the hell you went through, the people who hurt you, the people you lost. You'd think someone who got through all that and lived to tell about it wouldn't be so goddamned innocent."

"I'm not innocent," Eric protested. "I'm just minding my own business."

"Not according to Shaw. Ben Vaughan is nothing but a dumbass tool, but he's still Henry Shaw's son-in-law and Henry owns this town in every way that counts. If Shaw decides to mess with you, you will be messed with. I can't help you. He made that clear to me last night. You've got your head up your ass. So damn stupid."

"Not exactly stupid," Mace broke in helpfully. "Cum-poisoned. Different cause, same effect. Much higher fun factor. But hey, if you're going to ruin your whole life and get flattened by Fate, at least make it count, bro, am I right?"

"Zip it," Eric said, through his teeth. "I'll be late for work—"

"You'll lose the work," Otis said. "All of the work. No Shaw's Crossing employer in their right mind would go against that girl's granddad. I guarantee it."

"I hear you," Eric growled. "Don't flog a dead horse."

"So don't kill the damn horse!" Otis retorted. "You need that horse!"

Eric backed toward the door. "I have to go," he repeated.

"Eric." Otis's voice stopped him. "I said this years ago, but it looks like I need to say it again. If you get into trouble, or hurt someone, or run with garbage and get blamed for their smell, whatever it is, know this. If you end up on the wrong side of the law, I will cut you loose. No explanations. No excuses. No bail. No lawyer. You're on your own, twisting in the wind. Do. Not. Blow it."

"I understand," Eric said.

Otis, Anton and Mace came out onto the porch as Eric wrangled the Monster into gear. He disliked turning his back on Otis like an ungrateful, disrespectful shithead.

But he couldn't explain himself, or defend himself. It was a done deal. He was taking Demi to a secret place to pleasure her beyond her wildest dreams. That was the plan, and he could not turn back from it. No one could ask him to. It just wasn't an option.

The roar of lust in his head was louder than any voice of reason could yell.

A cold fist clutched his belly as he drove away, watching the worried faces of his family getting smaller and smaller in the cracked rearview. It felt almost like fear.

The lust was stronger.

# 6

The buzzing finally penetrated Benedict Vaughn's brain. Barely audible, like a dying insect inside the locked drawer in his desk. He'd been instructed to keep the phone on his person, but that made him too anxious. And attracted too much attention.

Good thing he'd been in the office. He did not want to blow off this caller.

Benedict rummaged for the key to the drawer with hands that were slightly unsteady after his third Scotch. Four rings. Five. Six.

He finally got it out and hit 'talk.' "Hello? This is Ben Vaughan."

The pause before answering was loaded with silent menace. "Don't ever make me wait that long before you pick up again." The deep voice was deceptively soft.

"Ah, sorry. I was just in the middle of—"

"I don't give a fuck what you were doing."

"Ah…yes, of course. So what can I do for—"

"You have to ask?"

Ben floundered, fishing desperately for the right answer. "I just wondered if—"

"The Trask brothers are all in Shaw's Crossing together. Right now. That hasn't happened for five years, and I am not okay with it. You had one job, Benedict. One."

"They haven't shown any signs of wanting to go back up to GodsAcre," Ben said nervously. "They're just visiting Otis. So I don't think—"

"I did not pay you to think. I bailed you out of your mess. You owe me."

"And I'm very grateful," Ben said quickly. "But I—"

"Do not interrupt me. Thinking is not your strong suit. I paid you to do as you're fucking told. You're falling down on the job."

"But I—"

"Your daughter's been seen with Eric Trask. Holding hands. Kissing him."

"I've got the situation under control," Ben assured him.

"The last thing I need is for a Trask boy to decide to hang around here. Your job was to make them feel unwelcome. You were supposed to encourage them in every possible way to get the hell out of town."

"And I did!"

"Your daughter is opening her legs for him, Ben. Seems to defeat that purpose, wouldn't you say?" The man's oily tone made Ben as angry as he was afraid. Almost.

"She's not opening her legs," he protested. "I've already talked to her, and she—"

"So this wide open legs state of affairs bothers you. That's good, Ben. I'm glad you're bothered. It means our personal interests are aligned. He's as much a liability for your family's future as he is to my own private interests. So take care of it."

Ben opened and closed his mouth, at a loss. "Uh…do you actually want me to—"

"Don't ask me to do your job. Fucking earn the money I paid you. Money that kept you out of jail. Be creative. Solve the problem. Permanently. Do we understand each other?"

"Uh, yes," he faltered. "Of course. You don't have to worry about my…hello?"

The line was dead.

"Ben? Honey? Who were you were talking to?"

Elaine stood in the doorway. He'd been so flustered, he hadn't seen her open the door. "What did I tell you about bursting in here without knocking?"

Elaine winced, but did not back down. Her eyes flicked down to the Scotch glass, then to the phone in his other hand. "That's not your smartphone," she said.

"That's not your goddamn business!" He couldn't get the snarl out of his voice.

Elaine noticed fucking everything. He'd fallen in love with her for that. Her perceptive intelligence. Her brilliant green eyes. Then he realized, too late, what it meant to live with a woman whose big, intelligent eyes saw far too much.

Elaine knew the man she'd married all too well. That knowledge made him squirm. And his daughter was just like her. That same unflinching gaze that saw too damn much.

"It's just a work phone," he mumbled, sliding it into his pocket.

"It's a burner," Elaine said. "You don't use burners for work. And someone just hung up on you. That didn't sound like a work call. You've gotten calls like that before. Who is it, Ben?"

"It's work!" he reiterated. "The line got disconnected.

It's nothing to worry about. Don't be paranoid. And don't spy on me. It's annoying."

She just kept looking at him. It was driving him crazy. "What?" he snapped. "Say it!"

"I got another call from Raelene," Elaine said.

Shit. Here it came. He braced himself. "Yes? What does she have to report?"

Elaine's mouth flattened. "She said that Demi left with Eric again. That wreck of a car he drives was parked down the street. She went straight for it. Made out with him in his car, right on the street in front of everyone, and then they drove away. So she's out there with him now. Somewhere."

Fury almost drowned out the dread, fogging his vision with red. Selfish slut. Spitting in his face. Throwing herself away on that piece of garbage just to spite him. After all the opportunities she'd been given. The privileges. That snotty, ungrateful bitch.

"I told Raelene not to call me with any more news like this," Elaine said.

"What?" he was horrified. "Why? That's insane! We need to monitor her!"

"No, I think not, Ben. Spying on her like that. It's wrong. She's an adult, whether we approve of her choice of boyfriends or not. God knows, I can hardly blame her. They just don't make them any better-looking than that young man."

"Have you gone nuts?"

"Not at all." Elaine's chin went up. "I'm trying to be fair. I'm also trying to salvage our relationship with our daughter, which is more than you're making any effort to do. Eric Trask…well, I don't know. Maybe he's not so bad. He's served his country, he's working hard, he's keeping his nose clean. He had a tough start in life, so hats off to him for trying to make something of himself. Maybe we should try giving him a fair shot."

The red fogged swelled. "I will not smile and nod while my daughter soils herself with that low-life filth!"

Elaine recoiled, eyes wide. "Ben! Control yourself!"

Ben flung his empty liquor glass at the wall. It hit a framed family portrait of the three of them, cracking the glass. Broken glass scattered over the Persian rug below. "You're ready to roll over? Let her flush herself down a toilet at the age of twenty-two? You're her mother, Elaine. How could you think that way?"

"Ben, you're overreacting. I simply said that he wasn't such a—"

"He was raised by a goddamn psychopath!" he yelled. "He's twisted. Do you want to breed that into your family line, Elaine? Because I don't."

She backed away toward the door, horrified. "Ben." Her voice had a nervous quaver. "You're forgetting something fundamental. You can't stop her."

"Oh, I'll put a stop to it, all right."

"How?" she demanded.

Fear grew in her eyes as the silence after her question got heavier.

"Oh, Ben," she whispered. "You wouldn't do anything illegal, would you? Because that's a point of no return, you know. We've talked about that."

"Don't be melodramatic," he snapped. "I need to think, and you're not helping. Go away. And fucking knock before you come into my office again. We've talked about that, too. Remember, Elaine? Boundaries? They go both ways."

He pushed her out the door, but Elaine just stood there,

holding her ground. "Do not do anything stupid, Ben," she said. "You've reached your quota."

He slammed the door shut between them to block out the fear in her eyes.

# 7

Demi tossed her knapsack into the back seat of the Monster and got in. Eric pulled her into a passionate, sensual kiss before she could say a word.

Brazen seduction, right out in front of everyone. He felt so good. His lips were soft and hot against hers. Tasting her, coaxing her to open. Making her boneless, breathless.

His kiss felt urgent. As if he were trying to persuade her of something, with all his wiles. Hah. As if she weren't already convinced. She was so completely hooked by him.

A horn honked as the car went by. She heard snickering and the occasional shocked gasp as people passed the open car window, but she didn't care. All that mattered was that shining connection. The wild excitement. Terrified joy spreading through her whole being, filling her up. Flowing over like a fountain. So hot. So sweet.

*Too soon. Cool it, girl. Calm it down. These feelings. They are out of hand.*

Someone thumped the hood of the car. "Get a room," a guy called out.

Eric pulled away, breathing hard. "Oh, man. Sorry. I'm like dry tinder. Go up like a torch as soon as I touch you. Hey…we could, you know."

"Could what?" She couldn't follow his train of thought. Her wits were scrambled.

"Get a room. Like the guy said. It'll take us maybe forty minutes to get to the place I wanted to show you. There'll still be some sun on the water. But if you don't feel like hiking, we could just drive up to the Ponderosa Motel at Granger Valley, or anywhere else you want, and just loll on a bed together. That would rock, too. You decide."

She pressed her hand against his shirt, which was hot and damp. "I've gotten attached to the romantic secret waterfall fantasy."

"Me, too. But now I'm attached to the hotel room, too. That can be our next tryst."

"Great."

He took the turn-off to the road leading up Kettle River Canyon, and she was taken aback. "Wait. Isn't this the way up to GodsAcre?"

"Yeah, but we're stopping well before that and hiking down to the water," he said. "Don't worry, I'm not taking you anywhere near that place. My brothers and I don't go up there. For love or money."

She shivered as if a cold wind had blown through her. "I should think not."

After a few miles of the Monster bouncing and shuddering over the rough, narrow road, Eric pulled off onto an even smaller and rougher logging road, thickly overgrown with long mountain grass. He parked the Monster in a grassy space behind a stand of sapling firs, and smiled at her. "Ready to walk?"

"Hell, yeah. I'm so curious."

Eric insisted on shouldering her bag along with his own, and led her onto an almost invisible deer trail that snaked through the trees down the hillside to the Kettle River. It roared and leaped between deep fissures of rock, and they jumped from one huge, flat slab of water-smoothed rock to another. At one point, they hopped all the way across to the other side of the river. It was too noisy to talk.

They came to the mouth of a smaller torrent that drained into the Kettle River. From there, Eric led her up that stream and into a mossy canyon that got increasingly taller, more shadowy. Dripping, secret and hushed, like a magical portal to another world.

They walked alongside the stream until there was no longer any place to walk, just steep walls hung with moss and green feathery tufts of foliage. The narrow stream rushed between, swift and silent and crystal clear, the water a startling pale blue-green.

"We have to go into the water to continue on," he said. "Put anything you're wearing that you need to keep dry into your bag. I'll put it all up on my head."

"It's that deep?"

"Up to my chest at least," he said. "And I've gone in when it was neck deep."

Huh. That would be over the eyebrows for her.

Demi had a self-conscious moment when she stripped off the tank and cut-offs she'd put on after her shift, revealing the skimpy moss green bikini. She'd chosen it this morning for the boob-hoisting balcony bra-effect, and the French cut bottom with ribbon ties had looked very come-hither in the mirror. But in this remote place full of shadows and murmuring water, it made her feel naked and vulnerable.

Eric's hot gaze heated her right up. He pulled off his work boots and clothes, revealing an impressive hard-on that made her face burn. Her come-hither bathing suit had done its appointed job. He was stiff and thick and full. Ready for action.

Her breath got all choppy and uneven just looking at him. Whew.

Eric packed his stuff and hers both into his battered bag, balanced the whole thing on top of his head, and waded into the stream. He made only a sharp intake of breath as the water closed around his chest and turned to her, holding out his hand.

She took it, and let him tug her in after him. "Oh, God," she moaned. "So cold."

Her hair fanned out around her on the surface of the water. Eric let go of her hand, stroking a long curling lock of it slowly and reverently before taking her hand again.

"No distractions," he said. "The sun won't last forever. Let's race for the light. Twilight comes early this far down in the canyons."

The current wasn't as overwhelming as the larger, noisier Kettle River, but it was still strong, and she couldn't touch the bottom. She swam along one-armed, but they made progress only because she was being towed by Eric. The shock of cold soon faded, and after a few minutes, she felt smooth pebbles and sand beneath her feet again.

She climbed up into a tumbled heap of boulders and stared around, astonished.

They were inside a big granite bowl, one side of which was cloven by a waterfall. Not huge or high, but the stream of water refracted off all the many crystallized striations of stone, creating a dreamy, flounced chiffon effect like a fairy's diaphanous skirt.

She was enchanted. Yellow water-loving flowers bloomed around the pool, wet with spray. The sides of the canyon were carpeted with thick moss and hanging plants. The last rays of sun slanted through trembling green leaves, making rainbows in the mist.

"I've never seen anything so perfect," she said.

Eric looked pleased with himself. "I know, right? Haven't seen it in years. I don't know if it has an official name, but I don't really care. Anton and Mace and I named it Lindsay Falls, for our mom. She died a few months after we found it."

Demi wound her fingers into his. "I'm sorry," she said. "When was that?"

"The winter before the fire," he said. "I was fifteen. Pneumonia. Just a stupid cough that wouldn't go away. She kept on saying she was fine. Until she wasn't."

"That's awful," she said.

"Yeah, it was bad. The beginning of the end for us."

"Yeah? How so?" She waited for more.

He shook his head. "GodsAcre wasn't always a nightmare. Back in the old days, back when Jeremiah was relatively lucid, there were good times, good things. But after Mom died, he lost it. He'd never been what you might call stable, but she grounded him, as much as anyone could. When she was gone, he came apart."

"Was he your real dad?" she asked, timidly.

"Not biologically. We moved to GodsAcre when I was four, and my mom hooked up with Jeremiah pretty soon after that. But he's the only father I remember, besides Otis. Otis definitely counts. He's a ballbreaker, but he's a great guy."

"Yeah, Otis is pretty awesome," she agreed.

"He's pissed at me right now," Eric told her. "For going after you. Thinks I'm miles out of my league."

She was startled. "Good God. Otis knows about us?"

Eric laughed. "Everyone knows about us."

She almost told him that she was in the same boat, but quickly thought better of it. This was not the moment to tell him how her parents thought he wasn't good enough.

Screw them. They would not ruin this for her.

But Eric was like an antenna, picking up every thought that flashed through her mind. "You, too?" he asked. "I take it your folks are less than thrilled about me."

She shrugged. "They have a narrow vision of what my life should be, and you don't fit into it. But to be honest, I don't fit into it either. So screw it. I can't please them no matter what I do, and I'm not going to hurt myself trying."

There was a moment of silence, punctuated only by birdsong and rushing water. The ray of sunlight sliced through the rippling water. Tiny white butterflies wafted around. Blue dragonflies hovered over the surface of the water.

Demi reached behind herself. Unhooked her bathing suit top. Tossed it onto the rock next to the bag. She just stood there, breasts bare, cheeks pink.

"Fortunately, none of the haters are here," she said. "We're alone."

Eric swallowed several times, staring at her. "Demi," he said. "You're so fucking beautiful."

She studied the streak of angry color on his cheekbones. His cock, straining against the wet boxers. Every detail of his fabulous erection clearly visible.

She stepped out of the bikini bottom, tossed it down to join the top, and flaunted herself shamelessly, in all her naked glory. She'd never felt so brazenly sure she wanted this. She wanted to provoke him, inflame him, drive him fucking crazy.

It worked. They came together without a word, kissing ravenously. Cool wet skin to cool wet skin. Blazing heat just beneath. She ran her hands over his shoulders. She could barely get a grip, they were so taut and thickly muscled.

She wound her arms around his neck and hung on for dear life. The magic seized them, like it always did. She knew that she should slow this down. Put the brakes on.

She couldn't. Not when her heart was opening up like this. The soft twisting ache, feelings coming alive, bursting into full color inside of her. Body and soul, calling to him straight from the heart. No lies. Nothing hidden. Nothing held back.

Hearts didn't lie. They couldn't.

*But they could break.*

She shoved that random unwanted thought away as Eric lifted his head. "Come to the edge of the pool," he urged. "Let me show you the perfect place."

The rocks around the pool were ground and polished by eons of winters and tumultuous springs, polishing the rocks to silky smoothness. The one he led her to was wonderfully warm, with all the day's stored sunshine in it. She perched on the edge, sliding her legs into the water. Eric got into the pool and came around to face her, hip deep.

He placed his hands on her knees, stroking them, asking a question with his body and waiting for an answer, though they both knew the answer already. It felt like a ceremony. The careful reverence of his slow touch. His patient waiting.

Enough. She opened her legs and clasped his waist with them. Reached down to stroke the stiff, dark red cockhead poking out of the waistband, right above the surface of the water. Gripping, stroking. There was pre-come on the tip. She made her hand slick with it, rubbing his blunt tip slowly in her palm. Squeezing and milking his thick shaft.

They groaned against each other's mouths as they kissed, shaking with need.

Eric sank down into the water, pressing his face to her breast. He slid his tongue around her nipple and followed with deep, tender suckling pulls, drawing pleasure up from inside her, endless shining waves of it.

The sweet sensations sharpened and grew. She hung onto his shoulders, gasping for air, until everything coalesced into a blinding flash of pleasure.

It throbbed through her. Deeply, endlessly. Melting her.

When her eyes opened, they were wet. She blinked at the smeary blur of blue, green, gold, black. The cliffs were tinted with sunset gold. Pine and fir ringed the edge.

She wiped the tears away and pulled him closer, pressing her face against his head. Nuzzling and kissing his thick, buzzed-off hair. It was damp and salty.

"Eric," she whispered. "Wow. That was crazy wonderful."

"Agreed." He lifted his head, awestruck. "You're so responsive."

"It's you," she informed him, and then clung to his upper arms as he shifted her, pushing her gently onto her back. The heat of the smooth rock was a caress against her skin. "What are you doing?"

He lifted her legs out of the water and put her heels against the edge of the rock, spreading her knees. "Pushing my luck," he said.

Her breathless laughter cut off as he sank down between her legs and put his mouth to her.

Oh, he was so good. Amazingly good, pressing light, flirtatious kisses against her mound while he petted her pussy lips with his fingertips, making her crazy with shivering excitement before he teased her pussy lips open, stroking and caressing. Sinking his finger slowly inside her slick channel while he ran his tongue over her clit. Back and forth, flicking and fluttering. Sucking on it tenderly, running his tongue around…and around it.

He was so aware of everything she felt. Every stroke, every pull, every lapping stroke of his tongue was exactly what she desperately needed, and then somehow it changed into something still more perfect. And again. And again. Tireless. Relentless.

He sucked tenderly on her clit and thrust his fingers inside her, finding with unerring skill all the inside places to stroke and pet, then doubling down and loving on them with passionate skill. Deeper when she needed it. Faster, when she craved it. Driving her straight for it—oh please…*please.*

*Yes.*

The climax was so huge, it made the world disappear in a blaze of wild perfection.

When the sensations eased back down to a shivery glow, she opened her eyes. She had no idea how long he had been waiting for her.

She smiled at him. "Sex god," she whispered.

He looked pleased. "It's amazing with you. It just takes me over. I can just…I don't know. Feel you. Like we're connected. I've never felt anything like it. It's magic."

"Aw. I bet you say that to all the girls."

"Hell, no," he said forcefully. "By no means do I say

that to all the girls."

She traced his gorgeous cheekbone with her finger. "What about you?"

He rubbed his face against her hand like a cat being petted. "What about me? I'm blissing out. I've got your sweet taste on my mouth. I've got you wet and wide open, trusting me with your body. Coming for me like crazy. Doesn't get any better than that."

"No?" She propped herself up onto her elbows and spotted the condom he'd left lying on the rock beside them. She picked it up and flapped it at him. "You tease."

The flush in his face deepened. "I didn't mean to tease. I just didn't want you to feel pressured. I want you to be ready. Whenever it happens is fine."

"Now would be good," she told him. "I'm so ready, Eric. Believe me, I wouldn't be lying here bare naked with my legs wrapped around you if I wasn't."

Eric took the condom from her and ripped it open. "You want me, you got me." He pulled her up until she was sitting and handed it to her. "Do the honors. I stand ready."

She seized his penis. So hot. Pulsing in her grip. It gave her an incredible thrill. A sense of raw power, knowing how much pleasure she could give his big, gorgeous body. How intensely he wanted to be inside her.

He squeezed his eyes shut, head dropped back as she milked him with her hand. Every slow, twisting stroke dragging a groan from his throat. Tendons stood out on his neck. His grip on her waist tightened. "Demi." His voice was pleading.

"You like it? Want some more?" She ran her thumb around the blunt tip of his penis, spreading silky pre-come round. Making him slick, so she could pump harder.

His stiff cock pulsed with eagerness in her hands.

"You're gorgeous," she told him. "All of you." She punctuated her statement with a bold, squeezing stroke that forced out more pre-come, dipped her fingers in it and brought them to her lips. "Yum," she whispered. "Sweet. Salty. Hot. Perfect."

"You, too," he said hoarsely.

She twisted her fist around his shaft. "Switch places with me and let me give you a taste of your own medicine," she urged him. "You won't regret it."

"After," he said. "I want to come inside you first."

Getting the condom on was tricky. Her fingers shook with excitement, and the tip of his big phallus was very thick. After a few awkward snap-backs, she finally managed to smooth it over him, with long, voluptuous strokes from root to tip. She loved the choked sounds he made with every swiveling pull of her hand. She just couldn't get enough.

She lay back on the warm slab of rock, offering herself as he stroked himself against her pussy lips. Sighing with pleasure as he caressed her clit with it.

He nudged himself inside, making himself slick and wet, then pushed slowly deeper. The sensation was so intense, she cried out.

He stopped instantly. "Am I hurting you?"

Demi tried to speak, licked her lips, cleared her throat. She shook her head, and dragged him closer, gasping out a single word. "More."

# 8

Fuck, yeah. Plenty more. As much as she wanted. Anytime, anywhere, forevermore. He was her man.

His soul shook. He'd never seen anything so perfect. The colors of her. The textures. Nothing existed soft enough, bright enough, smooth enough to compare to her. Those full pink lips. Her brilliant eyes seemed even greener with the reflection of the sky and the blue-green water. Her smooth belly and the sexy swell of her hips. Those plump, full, gravity-defying tits. The stark contrast of her bikini tan made him crazy with lust. She was golden tan, but for those creamy pale tits bouncing with each thrust. And the bikini bottom paleness around the trimmed up swatch of hair above her pussy.

He'd been so proud of himself, making her come just by sucking on her tits. Score one. Now he was hypnotized by the erotic spectacle of her shining pink pussy lips kissing his shaft as he inched inside her. Her tender inner lips were distended around his dick, shining with her juice. She was so perfect. Every fucking thing about her. Perfect.

He wanted to do everything at once. Make her come with his hands, his mouth, his dick. He wanted to make a goddamn impression. No effort spared. No shortcuts.

This was the real deal. She would get the very best of him. She always would. He'd be better than he'd ever aspired to be for her, because she fucking deserved the best, and he wasn't letting go of her. His only option was to rise to the challenge. Be good enough for her somehow.

All in. Balls deep. So perfect, the snug grip of her pussy around his shaft.

"You're tight," he muttered as he withdrew. "I don't want to hurt you. Gotta take this slow."

She shook her head, mouthing the word. *No.*

"No, what?" He went still. "Is it good for you? Do you want me to stop?"

"Don't you dare." Her nails dug into his chest, his shoulders, yanking him close. Stinging kitten claws. "More. Deeper. *Now.*"

That fierce, sexy glow in her eyes demanded everything he had.

Something inside him gave way. It was like a landslide, huge and unstoppable. He gave it to her. Nothing held back.

Demi lifted herself against his deep, hard thrusts, gasping with pleasure. Her pussy was like an exotic flower, all different shades of pink, leaving a fresh slick of lube on his penis with each plunging stroke. He pulled up the hood of her clit, making it pop out so he could play with the taut little button of sensation while he fucked her.

Her body stiffened with pleasure. "Eric," she breathed. "Oh my God..."

Something was happening to him. He was melting into her. Hanging on as hips bucked and heaved. They both made helpless, animal sounds. Hearts galloping, souls touching. Brighter and brighter.

Until there was nothing but light.

He collapsed on top of her after the pleasure had its wild way with him, panting. His hot face pressed to her breasts. Her arms were still twined around his neck. Her legs, squeezing him, keeping him clasped inside herself. He loved how lithe and strong she was.

The realization came to him slowly. He had no idea if he'd made her come. He'd been lost in his own personal supernova. Damn. After all his smooth lover-boy posturing, he just lost his mind the second he got inside her. Like a bumbling virgin.

He lifted his head. Her eyes were closed, but she had a beatific smile on her face.

That was a good sign. Please, God. "Are you, uh, okay?" he asked, cautiously.

"Didn't you hear me yelling?" she murmured. "I'm hoarse now. I think my throat might have cracked."

"I was too busy yelling myself," he admitted.

Her laughter sounded lazy with satisfaction. She stretched luxuriously, squeezing her legs around him. Her pussy clenched deliciously around him.

*Fuck* yeah. His cock leaped freshly to attention inside her, as if he hadn't just had the most mind-blowing orgasm of his entire life.

Demi's eyes popped open. She blinked at him. "Whoa," she said. "Already?"

"You're the most beautiful woman I've ever seen. Sorry. Can't help it."

He forced himself to withdraw his hopeful dick out of that hot, clinging paradise, holding the condom firmly on himself as he sank down into the water, trying not to pant. Trying to cool down and rinse off the sweat before climbing out to deal with the latex.

It hurt to look away from her. What a fucking waste, to turn his eyes away from the celestial vision of Demi Vaughan, wet, naked and smiling, even for a few seconds.

He made quick work of the condom, digging out the plastic bag he'd brought along for this purpose and wrapping it up for disposal later.

When he turned back to her, Demi had stretched out on one of the flat granite slabs, spreading her masses of drying hair around her on the rocks. Stretching, putting her arms back behind her head. Ribs tilted up. Legs parted. Giving him just a teasing glimpse of her pussy. She was showing off for him. Oh, man. He was so owned.

He laid down beside her. Demi's gaze flicked appreciatively down to his stiff-as-it-ever-was cock. "No condom? What's that about? Aren't you game for another round?"

He shook his head. "Not so soon." He bent down to press a tender kiss against her mound. "You're small and tight. You'll get sore if we overdo it. Next time around."

"I'm fine," she said. "I'm great. I love it."

"I said I'd be gentle and I wasn't," he told her. "I lost it. And I'd lose it again. I know it. Being inside you totally fucks with my self-control."

"Well, you losing control evidently works for me. It was amazing."

"Thank God." He slid his hand up the inside of her thigh, marveling at the perfect, flower-petal smoothness of her skin.

"This place feels magic," she said. "It's another

dimension, outside of time. We could stay for hours and when we went back, no time will have passed in the outside world. It's like none of my problems can bother me here."

"What problems are those?"

She shook her head. "You know. The classics. My family. All over my ass."

"About me," he said grimly. "I hate it that I made problems for you."

She laughed. "Whoops, there you go again! Making it all about you."

"Isn't it?"

"They are uptight about you, I can't deny it," she admitted. "But they think you're a symptom of a larger problem. You know, my general rebellion. Changing my major to the three-year restaurant management program. The internship. Saying no to Shaw Paper Products. The Culinary Institute. There was money put aside for my education when I was a baby, thanks to Granddad, but he controls access to it, and my parents think my idea of being a chef is childish and frivolous. That I'm chasing a TV celebrity fantasy. Now it looks like they've persuaded Granddad, too, and he was my last hope."

He waited. "So? What's next?"

She shook her head. "I do it on my own," she said. "All that's changed is my timetable. I'll put off chef school until I save money. I'll work lots of jobs, like you do. I'll be a paralegal by day, I'll do catering gigs by night. Whatever I can put together that pays the most. When I finally do go to chef school, I'll borrow the rest. I'll figure it out somehow."

"Where is this internship, anyhow?"

"The restaurant is in Seattle," she told him. "A person can make money in Seattle if she's willing to bust her ass."

"That's true," he said.

There was a brief pause while his mind raced. Then he opened his mouth and the words just fell out. "We could go to Seattle together."

The words reverberated between them. When he found the courage to look at Demi's face, her eyes were big. Almost frightened.

"Um…I don't know what to say," she said, her voice tentative.

"It doesn't matter where I go when I leave this town," he said. "Any place would do as well as any other. I was thinking about the desert. Albuquerque, or Vegas, where Anton is, but it makes no difference. With a satellite connection, I can do what I need to do with a phone from the top of the Himalayas. I could go to Seattle. Why the hell not?"

"But…what do you mean by going to Seattle? Exactly?"

"I mean we could go together," he told her. "Find a place. Live together. Be together. You do your thing, I do mine. But we help each other."

"Eric," she whispered. "Did you, ah…did you just ask me to move in with you?"

He pondered the question as the momentum swiftly built inside him. "Yes," he said. "Yes, I did just ask you that. And the more I think about the idea, the more I like it."

Demi in his apartment. Cooking with her. Fixing her car. Shopping with her. Walking with her. Watching movies with her. Hiking in mountains and rainforests with her. Getting into bed with her every night, waking up with her every morning. Yeah.

Oh hell, yeah. That idea was fucking brilliant.

"Dude," she said carefully. "You do realize that aside from a few weeks of smoldering eye contact, we've only known each other for a couple days, right? High school doesn't count. I ogled you from afar. We never even spoke."

"I knew the second I walked into the sandwich shop," he told her.

Demi just swallowed, gazing at him with those beautiful, searching green eyes.

"Am I fucking up the timing?" he asked. "Anton gives me hell about that. I know what I want when I see it. I don't change my mind. I don't see the point in wasting time once I've come to a conclusion. Why dick around when you're sure?"

"Yay for you, that everything is so clear-cut and obvious," she said. "Me, I need to work up to things a little more slowly."

"That's fine," he assured her. "Work up to this all you want. Take all the time you need. Just let me keep making you come while you're thinking about it."

She let out a crack of laughter. "Oh, come on. You're so bad."

"I just want you to be fully aware of the range of my potential usefulness to you," he said innocently. "I have many gifts. They would all be at your service. Day and night."

"That's evident, from the looks of you," she said, smiling at his hard-on.

"I'll never get enough of you," he told her. "You're so beautiful. I'd be hot for sex all the fucking time. But I'd try to be classy and grown-up about it, I swear to God."

"Um, about that," she said in a teasing voice. "We could have another go. Right now at this moment, I mean. I'm so ready. I'd love it."

Eric's breath locked up in his chest as she opened her legs, sliding her own fingers inside her pussy lips. Opening them for him. Showing him the shining pink inside bits. So tender and yielding. His dick jerked, aching with eagerness to forge back inside that plush warmth and fuck wildly. All the way to the explosive finish.

No. He needed to demonstrate self-control. Coherence. He was in this for the long haul. And it was too…fucking…soon for her. This was so damn hard. It killed him.

"Next time," he said, through clenched teeth. "Don't tempt me."

"Aw, you're no fun." She pouted playfully and rolled onto her side. "You're not how I thought you would be."

"Huh?" he demanded blankly. "How did you think I was?"

"Oh, you know. Girls talk."

He went suddenly tense. "Do they? What do they say?"

"That you've got amazing technique, for starters," she said. "They also say that you're a bang-em-and-bounce type. The kind that loses interest and moves on as soon as he makes a conquest. And here you are, asking me to run away with you."

"Lose interest? In you?" His voice cracked with disbelief. "You're kidding, right?"

"It happens." She smiled, closing her eyes. Stretching luxuriously. Displaying her breasts for him as her back arched.

He stretched out next to her. "So that's my rep. Soulless man whore. Who knew."

"Not soulless," she corrected. "Voracious. Tireless. Easily bored."

"Not by you," he assured her. "When I know I'm being used, I use right back, for sure. But you never made me feel that way."

"Used for what? Sex?"

He laughed under his breath. "Not for money or status, that's for damn sure," he said, his voice ironic. "Sex, yeah. Entertainment. Excitement. To punish ex-boyfriends or jealous husbands. To carve a notch or scratch an itch. Banging the bad boy made them feel dangerous and naughty and powerful. In those conditions, yes. I do bore easily."

"I thought you said you liked dangerous."

"I know when it's an act," he said. "With you, it's different. You're for real. And me asking you to go to Seattle with me? That's not just a slick line to get laid. Believe it."

"Eric—"

"That's a rock solid offer. I've never made a realer one in my life." He pulled her hand to his lips and kissed it reverently. "I'd follow you anywhere, Demi Vaughan."

Her eyes dropped. "I think we should slam the brakes on your imagination for a while," she said demurely. "Let's take this a day at a time. Just see how it goes."

Again, he'd overdone it. His older brother would laugh his ass off. Tell him he was being greedy and impatient. Grabbing for more before the time was right.

*Just breathe, dude. And wait.* That was what Anton always said.

Eric rolled onto his back and stared up at a red-tailed hawk that soared across the sky above the bowl of stone. He didn't allow himself to speak until the bird had vanished behind the ragged curtain of trees on the cliff top above. Breathing and waiting.

"Okay," he said. "I'll slow down." *But I won't stop thinking about it. Every minute.*

The words he didn't say felt louder than the ones he

spoke aloud.

"Come on." Demi sat up, fluffing out her tangled hair. "Don't be that way."

"What way?"

"You know, all quiet and sulky. Come on, Eric. We should wait to put both our names on a lease at least until after we've had our first fight, don't you think?"

He laughed under his breath. "I'm not sulking," he assured her. "I'm just making an attempt at self-control. You know, trying to play it cool. Trying not to fuck this up."

"You're not very convincing. And you're projecting a very powerful frequency."

"Sorry," he said simply. "This is just how I am. This is new for me."

"What? Ill-considered, rash proposals to girls you barely know?"

"Exactly," he agreed. "I've never done it before. Asked a girl to be with me seriously, I mean. I don't even do second dates. But you're different. The way this feels…I didn't even know this was an option. And now that I know, I can't go back. I can't settle for less. Ever again."

Her eyebrows went up. "Eric," she murmured. "Who would have thought you'd be such a romantic."

"If I go for something, I go all the way," he said. "And I never give up."

There was a brief, awkward silence. He realized, appalled, that he'd done it again. Even worse this time. The more he tried to restrain himself, the more over-the-top intense the words that came out of his mouth became. So much for breathing and waiting.

*Shut up, Trask. Shut your fucking trap before you blow it.*

He got up, pulling on his wet shorts. "We'd better go,"

he muttered. "The sun's gotten low. We don't want to do that path in the dark."

# 9

Run away with him? Holy *crap.*

Demi was as tongue-tied on the way back as she had been on the trip out, but for entirely different reasons. Before, she'd quivered with breathless anticipation. Wondering if sex with him could possibly live up to her feverish expectations.

Now she knew.

She swam after him down the long sweep of canyon, much faster now that they were floating with the current. The channel was darker, and more mysterious in the fading light of evening. She was dazzled by the shadowy beauty of it. The feelings raging through her.

She was under his spell. She wanted deeper, more, always. Dangerous thoughts that led to dangerous places. She knew better than to go off the deep end with wild romantic fantasies like this.

They dried off and put their clothes and shoes back on when the narrow channel through the sheer canyon widened out to scattered boulders again. The rock-hopping part of the walk required her complete attention, but Eric kept looking back to make sure she was close behind, every time flashing her a smile that made her knees weak.

*Get a freaking grip, girl.* Her idea had been to grab a guilty little taste of paradise. One last special treat before launching herself into this new, challenging part of her life.

But…running away with him to Seattle? Holy. Bleeping. *Crap.*

It was crazy. But once the idea took root, she started elaborating on it. Scenes of domestic and erotic bliss started to fill her mind. After Mom and Dad and Granddad's ultimatum, she'd been steeling herself for a lonely hero's quest out in the big wide world.

Having a fascinating sex god of a boyfriend along on her quest—boy, did that ever change the picture. That could be all kinds of fabulous fun. It beckoned. A siren song.

But it wasn't real, she reminded herself savagely. It was a pipe dream. She barely knew the guy. She had no idea if he kept his promises. If she'd hold his interest for long.

One thing was certain. She was drunk on sex and not thinking clearly. So *chill.*

As soon as the path was wide enough for two, he stopped and waited for her, taking her hand. His clasp felt good. Firm, warm. Not hot or clammy or clutching.

The contact sent a fresh flash of sensual energy up her arm that tightened her nipples and touched off a hot, yearning, melting ache between her legs. Of course.

It was almost dark when they reached the car. He opened the passenger side door for her, then got in the driver's side and just sat there. Not moving or speaking.

She waited until she couldn't stand the suspense. "What's wrong? Are you okay?"

"Yes," he said. "Just scared."

That gave her pause. "Scared? Of what?"

"Being this happy," he said roughly. "It feels dangerous. Like flying too close to the sun."

Tears stung her eyes. She blinked them back. "I know what you mean," she admitted. "I feel that way, too. Maybe we should, ah…you know. Cool it for a while."

"Yeah, maybe. I guess." They stared at each other.

He reached for her at the same moment that she reached for him and they came together hard, like they'd die if they didn't kiss right now, touch right now. She wrapped her arms around him. He lifted her onto his lap. There was just enough light to see the expression in his eyes. Raw emotion. It reached inside her, squeezed her heart.

Oh, to hell with it. She was not done with this guy tonight. Not by a long shot. She reached down, wrenching at the buttons of his jeans.

"Hey!" he protested. "Demi, I don't think we should—"

"Shhh. Help me get these open."

She reached inside his underwear, gripping him. So thick and hard and hot. She rubbed him, squeezing her legs around the thrill of intense erotic desire he provoked.

"Get those underwear down," she told him.

"Demi—"

"I don't feel like arguing," she informed him.

Eric laughed under his breath, and lifted his hips to shove down his jeans. His freed erection jutted up against his belly.

She stroked it lovingly. "You are so beautiful," she said.

"That's my line," he told her. "You're the gorgeous one.

There were so many responses she could make to that, she abandoned them all in favor of body language, simple and direct. She leaned down and licked the head of his penis.

Eric gasped, going rigid. "Oh, fuck. Demi."

"Relax," she whispered. "It's my turn. You owe me that."

"If you say so…oh God..."

He writhed, shaking as she gripped his rod firmly right under the head of his penis and gave him a lavish tongue-lashing. Twisting her hands on his shaft, swirling her tongue, cupping his balls. Flicking away each silky, salty drop of pre-come as it came out of the slit in his glans with her tongue. Savoring his flavor. He was delicious.

She loved that shuddering vibration. Like he was a volcano about to explode.

Taking him all the way into her mouth was quite a feat, but she was highly motivated. She wanted to destroy him with pleasure. Make him as desperate for her touch as she was for his. She sucked him deeper, sliding her hands along his whole length.

Eric slid his fingers into her hair at the nape of her neck and tugged gently.

"Can I come in your mouth?" he asked.

She slid her tongue up and down the underside of his shaft while she thought about it. Tough one. She wanted to say yes. Absolutely. She also wanted him inside her.

She wanted it bad. Wanted it *now.* "Where did you put the condoms?"

He hesitated before answering. "Uh, are you sure you want to—"

"Do I look unsure to you?"

He laughed under his breath and twisted back, stretching out his arm to rummage in the pocket of the bag in the back seat. He came forward with the box.

Demi ripped one open and pulled it out, rolling it over him. Stroking, squeezing, bold strokes that made Eric arch right up off the seat. "Holy fuck, Demi."

"Scoot over toward me," she said, dragging off her cut-offs and underwear.

Eric shifted over to the middle of the Monster's big, tattered bench seat, and she had barely enough room to swing her leg over his and straddle him.

Eric slid his hand up her inner thigh, stroking and petting. "You're so wet."

"Oh, yeah," she said. "Hold yourself up for me."

"Yes, ma'am."

"Smart-ass," she said breathlessly, until she felt his thick tip nudging inside her, right where she needed him.

She sank down, taking him in. All the way.

So deep. So wonderful. They both made the same shocked sound. Their eyes met, locked. Demi leaned her hot, damp forehead against his.

"You feel amazing," he whispered.

"Likewise." She rose up, and sank back down again with a sigh of delight. "You make me crazy."

"You're telling me." Eric pushed up her shirt, all the way over her breasts, and pressed his face against them.

They stopped talking, just clutching each other, as if they were fighting to get closer. His mouth moved all over her breasts, and his big hands clasped her ass cheeks, surging upward to thrust inside her. A slow, luscious pumping rhythm that made her helpless with need.

She melted around him. Each deep caressing stroke got sweeter, hotter, more frenzied than the one before. That uncontrollable energy swelled, lifting them—

They cried out as the blinding flash of pleasure fused

them into one.

She lifted her head afterward, feeling his hands on her face, cupping it. Stroking.

"I love you," he told her.

She stared back, her fingernails digging into his back.

She loved him, too. She ached to say it. But she held it back. That phrase was a point of no return. Too soon. She was risking her heart as it was. Walking a knife's edge.

Eric hid his face against her hair. He thrummed with energy. Demi lifted herself, and Eric let her go, hissing with reluctance as he dragged his dick slowly out of her.

"I love being inside you," he said. "I hate leaving."

The next few minutes were a scramble in the dark, trying to find her cutoffs and underwear in there, since the Monster had no functioning interior light. She finally had to dig out her phone and switch on the torch function to locate her stuff.

They wrestled their clothing back on in utter silence.

"So much for playing it cool," she said.

"Yeah," he agreed. "Like trying to put out a fire with kerosene."

They could no longer see each other's faces in the darkness, but they kept trying.

"Sorry," he said quietly.

"For what?"

"You know. Coming on so strong. Saying what I said. I know it's too soon. I mean, it's not too soon for me. I meant what I said one hundred percent. But I know it's too soon for you."

"It's okay," she said.

He slid his hands under her shirt, cupping her breasts. "All I ask is for you to make space in your mind for the idea of us." His voice was low and velvety soft. "Just picture us together. Imagine it. That's all."

She almost laughed. Like she could imagine anything else. He filled her whole mind.

"You don't have to say yes," he said. "Just picture us together. It would be good."

She nodded. Her throat had frozen tight. She couldn't talk.

The Monster roared to reluctant, sputtering life. Eric maneuvered it out onto the rough road and took her hand, letting go of it only to change gears.

When they got to her house, Eric pulled over in the shadow of the trees, well out of sight. The porch light was on and her father was visible in the upstairs window of his studies. Looking out at the street. Lying in wait.

"Shall I let you out here?" His voice was carefully neutral.

"There's no point," she said. "They know who I've been with all afternoon. Pull up right in front."

He gave her a searching look. "You sure? You're not using me to punish them, or anything twisted like that, right?"

She squeezed his hand. "Absolutely not. We've left that kind of thing behind us."

He revved the motor. "Okay, then. Let's do this." He pulled up in front of the house and killed the engine. "Shall I walk you up to the door and introduce myself?"

"I don't know if we're quite there yet," she said quickly. "I don't want him to be rude to you."

"I have a thick skin," he assured her.

"Not tonight. My skin is thin tonight. This is enough for now. Baby steps."

"Whatever. One thing, though. Just because it's

bugging me."

He got out of the car. She hurried to follow, feeling almost panicky, but he made no move to go toward the house. He headed over to the mailbox, still tilted over.

Eric then proceeded to hoist the mailbox upright, and kick gravel back into place around it, scooping first with his foot and then with his hands.

"There," he said, brushing off his hands. "That's better. Until the next time your lush of a neighbor goes off on a tear."

"Uh…thank you," Demi said, bemused.

Eric cupped her head and pulled her close for a swift, possessive kiss before getting back into the Monster. "I have my usual two hours between my shifts tomorrow. Every free second of it is yours, if you want it."

"Sign me up for that," she said. "I lay claim to all of it."

He waited as she walked to the front door, then flickered his headlights in farewell.

Demi lifted up her chin and marched into the house, bracing herself.

---

Any lingering uncertainty in Benedict Vaughan's mind vanished at Eric Trask's brazen display of insolence and disrespect. Parking that hideous wreck of a machine right in front of the house. Putting his hands on Benedict's property. Tongue-kissing his daughter in plain sight. Staking his claim, like an animal marking his territory.

Disgusting. But he expected no different from the Prophet's spawn.

The randy, arrogant bastard deserved whatever he got. Benedict was almost tempted to do the honors himself, but it was always better to consult a professional.

He had just the man, lined up and waiting. Benedict tested the door lock for the fourth time as it rang, just to be sure. He didn't want to be unpleasantly startled by Elaine. Not during this call.

The phone rang, and the line clicked open. "Yeah," said a sharp, nasal voice.

"It's on," Benedict said in a hushed voice. "Tomorrow. Could be night, could be morning. As soon as I know he's been moved into place, I'll call you."

"That's too big a time window," the voice complained. "I don't like sitting around waiting for a call. Kick in another five K for the wasted time."

"We already negotiated the fee. You said—"

"I don't give a fuck. Find someone else if you don't like it."

"I'll pay it," Benedict snapped.

"Leave it at the drop point tonight. No more calls. Not until it's time to mobilize. I'm tired of your voice. You talk too much."

The line went dead. Benedict slid the phone into his pocket. His stomach heaved.

"Ben?" Elaine's plaintive voice was right outside the door. "Demi's home. Why don't you come on down? We can discuss the thing we talked about over dinner."

Benedict unlocked the door and opened it. Elaine had that sugary-sweet look on her face that made him want to bang his head against a wall. Or better yet, hers.

He forced a smile for her benefit. "Hey, honey."

"You saw Demi arrive?"

"With Trask. Yes, I saw that. I imagine all the neighbors saw it, too."

"We're taking it easy, remember?" she said anxiously.

"You won't attack her, right? We have to keep those lines of communication open. Even if you think she's being provocative, just ease off. Some things she'll just have to learn for herself the hard way and that boy is probably one of them."

"Don't worry," he soothed. "I won't come down on her. I promise."

Elaine looked cautiously relieved. "Good, then. Come on downstairs, and we'll talk. Demi?" she sang out. "Sweetheart? Is that you?"

"Yeah, Mom." Demi appeared at the foot of the stairs.

"I would've appreciated a call to let me know you were going to be late. Your father and I have already had dinner, but there's a plate for you to microwave."

"Okay, sorry about that. Thanks, Mom. Maybe I'll have it in a bit."

Demi was stalled at the foot of the stairs, looking up at them. Her damp shirt clung to her body, and her hair still swung around her in wild, water-tangled locks.

"I see you went swimming again?" Elaine's voice had a fake-cheerful tone.

"Yes. Eric showed me a beautiful place he knows up Kettle River Canyon."

"That's very nice. So, ah, sweetheart. Your father and I are taking a trip."

Demi stopped climbing the stairs, raising startled eyes. "A trip? When? Where?"

"This weekend," Elaine announced. "Tomorrow. It was your father's idea, actually. We both need a little R&R. Too much stress lately."

"It's almost our anniversary," Benedict said. "We should do something special."

"It's a lovely idea," Elaine chimed in. "Cooper's Corner has a dinner theater. I found a nice bed and breakfast. We'll make a weekend of it. We can go up the ski lift to the viewing point, have lunch in the chalet café, some shopping in Cooper's Corner, and attend the dinner theater in the evening. A musical, I think. We'll leave tomorrow at noon."

"Ah, wow," Demi said. "That's great. Good for you. Go for it."

"You'll be all right here on your own, won't you, honey?"

Demi rolled her eyes. "I've been living by myself for years, remember?"

"Well, fine. In any case, your father asked Granddad to come over and check on you before he goes down to the Flats tomorrow morning. He'll be here at seven-thirty, so make sure you have some coffee and pastries ready for him."

Demi rolled her eyes. "That wasn't necessary, Mom."

The hell it wasn't. Benedict put on a benevolent smile by sheer force of will.

He was no longer the least bit conflicted about what he'd arranged. His stupid daughter had done this to herself with her own hands.

Besides, he was doing it for her, ultimately. Demi couldn't see how she was limiting her own future with this damaged, stunted, possibly even violent young man.

Eric Trask would stifle her, embarrass her, burden her. He would hold her back in every way.

This line of reasoning made him feel much better as he watched Demi disappear into her bedroom.

These desperate measures were all for Demi's sake.

His conscience was clear.

# 10

Home was uncomfortable, what with Otis's icy disapproval and the relentless shit he got from his brothers, so Eric packed it in early and retreated to his attic. He was exhausted, but something like a combat buzz wouldn't let him come down for a landing.

Dick-tingling images of Demi's body, mostly. The erotic flashbacks were intense, in perfect, full-sensory detail. Everything about her turned him on. He could meditate all night on the drops of water caught in her tangled eyelashes, and that was just for starters. The pale, back-lit jade green of her eyes, ringed with a band of darker gray. Clear, far-seeing. Honest. Blazing with desire.

Their connection was so strong. The taste of her sweet pussy folds against his tongue, and the feeling when she came right against his face. So damn good.

He wished he could text her. No cell coverage here. He was tempted to hike up onto the ridge where he could sometimes catch a wave. There might be enough moonlight to light his way up there. Keep him from tumbling over a cliff.

Except that it was the middle of the night. He'd be overdoing it again. *Cool it.*

Oh man. This was hell. Eric groaned under his breath, shifting around on the bed. His aching erection was trapped inside his sweatpants. The night was so damn long. He stared at the moonlight through the trees. Watched the hour hand crawling around the luminescent clock-face.

Around four he gave up the fight. The only advantage to insomnia was that he might actually make it out of there without any more shit from his family.

He couldn't take any more. He was a fucking raw nerve.

He burned to make a declaration to Demi, but he'd skated up very close to that today and succeeded only in scaring her half to death.

But that didn't mean he couldn't be fully prepared for the right moment when it finally arrived. Demi deserved for that moment to be absolutely perfect.

Eric threw on his clothes and dug into the lock-box under his bed where he kept his stash of earnings. He counted it out and shoved the lot into his jeans pocket. If he did this, he'd be setting back his professional plans by months.

Fuck it. Life was a series of sacrifices. That was one of old Jeremiah's truisms. Some of the stuff that Jeremiah had hammered into his head was paranoid bullshit. Some of it was spot-on.

For Demi, any sacrifice was worth it.

He coaxed the Monster into life and drove into town. Too early for work. Soon he found himself in Demi's neighborhood, driving up and down her street. Watching her house as the sun came up. It was stalkerish, but he wished he could pull a full-on Romeo. Throw a pebble at her window.

Spout poetry at her.

Better yet, he'd climb up into her window and drive her wild with pleasure in her own bed. He was a lot better with his body than he was with words.

But he didn't know which room was hers. He'd probably wake up Ben Vaughan and get shot in the face, and he'd deserve it for being such an idiot. Even texting her at this hour of the morning would come across as desperate and unhinged.

It took everything he had to hold himself back.

He got to work early, but it was hard as hell to concentrate today. He took the earliest possible lunch break and headed to the Bakery Café like a guided missile.

He craved the sight of her. Like oxygen.

Raelene gave him the stink-eye the second he walked in, but who the fuck cared, while Demi's beautiful smile was floating him right up off his feet. His heart swelled until he felt like there wasn't room inside his ribs for it to fit.

"Demi! I need you in the back right away!" Raelene brayed.

Demi beckoned him to the counter and passed him a folded up pink Post-It note. "I figured she'd say that as soon as you showed up," she whispered. "Sorry. Gotta go."

The faintest brush of her fingers against his aroused him. He watched her hurry into the back, throwing one last smile over her shoulder, and unfolded it, ignoring the other girls behind the counter asking for his order.

**My parents are gone for the weekend. The house is mine. Meet me there as soon as you get off work. Text me when you're parking your car.**

Excitement blasted through him. Whoa. Risky. Sneaking into the inner sanctum. Climbing into the princess's tower. He was so ready for that scenario, his dick ached.

He wandered out of the bakery café without ordering. He'd forgotten all about food. He just walked down the sidewalk, picturing her bed. Canopy, four-poster, wood, brass, who knew? Wide enough for two? Long enough for him? Pillows, ribbons, lace?

Didn't really matter. He didn't even need a bed. He only had a couple of hours until his shift at the care home anyhow, and a couple hours more in the morning after the shift ended. He sure as hell wasn't going to waste any of that precious time sleeping.

A glitter caught his eye, as the midday sunlight hit the display window of Steigler's Fine Jewelry. He came closer, studying the rings.

It was so soon for a ring. She was spooked already by the intensity of his conviction. But he could prepare, and then bide his time, perfectly positioned to blow her mind whenever the time was right.

Moments later, he was in the jewelry store. Trudi Steigler, a large, square woman in her fifties, was showing him engagement rings and watching like a hawk to be sure he didn't make off with them.

"I want something blue," he told her. "Maybe in white gold."

"I have some boulder opal rings set in white gold with diamonds. Some of them are blue. But they're in the Rhys Bryon Sea Change collection," Trudi told him. "Very high end."

"Can I see them?"

She pulled out a large case from a drawer behind herself, and opened it.

He saw Demi's ring instantly. Nestled in black velvet

on the far side. It was one of the smaller ones, set in white gold. An irregularly shaped opal ringed with tiny diamonds.

The stone was exactly the color he was looking for. When he turned it, light flashed through it, turning the blue to a startling backlit blue-green.

Just like rippling glacial melt water sparkling in the sun. The ultimate peak moment, immortalized in a gem. It was fucking perfect.

"How much for that one?" he asked, pointing.

Trudi peered at it, consulted a chart and named a sum that made his body contract.

For a second, he thought of going with a cheaper option, but those thoughts quickly spun themselves out. No, he didn't have the cash. Not yet. But that was the ring. No other ring would do. No question about it.

"I'm a few hundred dollars short," he told her. "Can I put it on layaway? Just for another few weeks. Another paycheck and I should be able to cover it."

Trudi looked disapproving, but her expression warmed when he pulled out the wad of cash from his pocket and began counting the hundreds out onto the counter.

"I suppose I can," she said, grudgingly. "Just fill this out."

She passed him a form, and he entered all the info she needed, and then walked out, almost completely broke.

He had only twenty-three bucks left in his pocket.

Sacrifice.

About an hour before it was time to leave work, Sy, his boss, came out of the trailer behind the building and called him. "Eric. Come on back here. Gotta talk to you."

He followed Sy into the trailer. Sy sat down at the desk, not meeting his eyes. "Sit down," he said heavily.

Eric's belly dropped. He knew trouble when he smelled it. He didn't bother sitting down. "What is it?"

Sy frowned down at his battered, thick-fingered hands and let out a sigh. "Eric. I'm, uh, gonna have to let you go."

What was left of his euphoria drained away as if a plug had been pulled inside him.

Consequences. Otis had warned him. Sacrifice. Jeremiah had warned him, too.

"Why?" Eric asked, just to make Sy squirm. He knew without being told.

"Well, uh…turns out I'm overstaffed." Sy looked everywhere except for at Eric. "And you know how it is. Last hired, first fired, so it's you who has to—"

"You hired Trevor and Kyle three weeks after me. And you put out a call for more workers just last week."

"Ah, yeah, well. In this business, you make hard choices, and I have to prioritize the people with the specific skills and experience that I need for—"

"I work better than anyone else on your crew," Eric said. "You said it yourself. Ricky, too, after I re-installed those door frames after Lorens fucked them up."

"Damn it, Eric," Sy blustered. "You've got a pretty fucking high opinion of yourself, you know that? I do not have to explain myself to you!"

"I have more skills than people here with twenty years of experience," Eric said. "You said the same thing to Anton when he worked for you. We were trained in woodworking, carpentry, mechanics, engineering. We've worked building crews since we were kids. You can't tell me it's my skills. Or my work ethic. I'm here early every day."

Sy slammed his hand down on the desk. "Maybe you should have worked harder on not pissing off the wrong people in this town! You think I like this situation?"

Eric blew out a slow breath. "You're getting squeezed? By Ben Vaughan?"

"Fuck Vaughan. I'm talking Henry Shaw, the grandfather. Got a call from his lawyer. I'm real sorry. It's true that you're a good worker, but you gotta go. Look for work outside of this town. You'd have better luck." He paused, and added, "Come to think of it, you should look for love outside of this town, too. If you want my opinion."

"I don't," Eric said stonily.

"Figured as much," Sy muttered. "For real, I'm sorry about this. But I can't afford to lose the convention center and Shaw is all over that project. What he says goes. Sorry, buddy. Also. If anyone asks, I never told you this. Anyone asks, and I deny everything and say I caught you using drugs on the job. So don't."

"Won't be necessary," Eric said.

"Just go," Sy said. "Don't come back for your last paycheck. I'll just send it to you at Otis's."

Eric walked out into the blazing heat. The smell of raw-cut wood and pine needles and fresh cement tickled his nose. Summer insects hummed loud in his ears.

He just stood there, contemplating his new situation.

Of all his jobs, this one had paid the most. Six steps back on the playing board.

On the plus side, he almost owned a white gold, opal and diamond ring from Rhys Byron's Sea Change Collection.

The whole thing would be almost funny, if it didn't suck so hard.

His phone rang. He pulled it out, hoping it was Demi, but no such luck. It was the care home. His guts thudded down another couple notches as he answered. "Yes?"

"Hi! This is Sandy Gottlieb, from Personnel at the Fair Oaks Care Home?" It was a bright, chirpy female voice. "Is this Eric Trask?"

"Yes, this is he," he said. "How can I help you?"

"Mr. Trask, I'm calling to inform you that we no longer have any shifts available for you to work going forward. So you don't need to come in tonight. Or in the future."

Sandy sounded so cheerful about it, it sounded almost as if she thought she was doing him a favor. "I see," he replied. "Can you tell me why?"

"Well, um, no. You'd have to speak to your direct supervisor about that. I was just informed of the decision, and I'm passing the information on to you. If you want to contest their decision, you'll have to call next week, from Monday through Friday during regular business hours, and we'll set up an appointment for you. Okay?"

"I understand," he said.

Sandy rattled on after an awkward pause. "Well, then! Have a great weekend, Mr. Trask! Buh-bye!"

He stood there for a moment, his mind blank, then put the phone in his pocket. When he pulled out his hand, two pieces of paper fluttered out onto the ground.

The receipt for the ring. The folded pink Post-It with Demi's invitation.

He picked them both up. Blankness was giving way to a slow burn of anger.

At this point, there was hardly even any point in calling the gas station to see if the same situation held true there. Of course it did.

He didn't want to tell Demi. Their connection was so new and tender, and he'd already stressed it by asking too much too soon. Something as heavy as this could crush it.

She didn't need to know. He'd just live the fantasy tonight. He didn't even have to cut short his time with her. He could settle in. Take the whole night. Do the thing properly.

Until she forgot she was the princess of Shaw's Crossing. By morning, she'd know that they were made to be together. Her parents and granddad could go fuck themselves.

Reality could wait. Her family's meddling, him leaving town, Otis's inevitable I-told-you-so, Mace's jibes, Anton's X-ray stares. All of it.

Kick it down the road until tomorrow.

When it came to kicking things down the road, alcohol helped. There was a liquor store down the block. He made for it, and settled on tequila. He liked the crazy edge of a tequila buzz. After he paid up, he still had a few bucks for limes at the grocery store.

Time to clean up. He got into the Monster, and headed to the Kettle River. Scrubbed himself up. Some deodorant, a fresh tee-shirt and jeans from the bag in the back seat, sandals to replace his heavy work boots, and he was good to go.

He pulled out the string of condoms from the box and stuffed them in his pocket, then rubbed some aftershave lotion he'd stowed in the car onto himself.

The thought of the night ahead made him burn. But he had to keep all this anger and humiliation out of his head when he was with her.

It occurred to him that tonight's plan just happened to be the perfect fuck-you, from his enemies' point of view. What better revenge than to steal into their ancestral home and nail their beautiful golden girl senseless right in her own frilly bedroom? He was scoring a point. Counting coup. He almost wished it could be that simple. That ugly.

But not him. He had to go and fall madly in love with her.

He parked around the corner, under a shaggy stand of pines, and texted.

**Here now. Got off work early. Don't have to go to the care home tonight.**

She took two seconds to respond.

**Awesome. Go around the lawn in the trees to the back of the pool house to avoid security cams. I'll meet you back there.**

He laughed to himself as he headed into the trees. True to form. Sneaking in through the back door. Like always, he was a guilty pleasure.

Fuck it. Who cared.

He'd focus on the pleasure.

# 11

Demi put on another slick of lip gloss and checked herself in the mirror one last time before hurrying through the house. She made her way out the kitchen door, through the big four-car garage, and from there to the storage sheds and the pool house.

Once out, she made her way carefully around the garbage cans, having studied the camera angles of her dad's security cameras' motion detectors in minute detail back in high school. She'd choreographed the best route to sneak in or out of the house without being seen or sensed, and it hadn't failed her yet.

Once out of range in the pine trees, she stood there in the dappled grove and stared around herself, waiting for Eric. The sun slanted through the pine and cedar boughs, hot and sultry. The air seemed tinted golden, perfumed with spicy pine, heavy, tangy sweet and nose tickling. She was surrounded by the deep, chittering hum of summer insects.

Where the hell was he?

She looked around and around. She should see him

from here from any direction by now. Maybe if she went down to the bottom of the hill—

"Hey." Eric's quiet voice was right behind her.

She spun around with a gasp, almost jumping out of her skin. He'd appeared out of nowhere. "Holy shit!" she gasped out. "You sneaked up on me!"

"Old training," he said. "Hard to break."

"You just appeared out of thin air. How did you do that?"

"I was taught how not to be seen since I was small," he said. "I thought you didn't want anyone to see me, right? The street, the neighbors, the cameras?"

She glanced over at the neighbor's house, barely visible in the distance. "I did not enjoy it when Raelene called my mom to tell her that I was with you," she said. "Nor do I want to have that conversation with my dad when he comes back. I've been craving some actual privacy. If I have to sneak around for it, so be it."

"I've had lots of practice with sneaking around," he told her. "I'm an old pro."

Demi paused, taken aback by his tone. He was as gorgeous as ever, but he seemed different today. His eyes looked distant. Remote. And he wasn't smiling.

She didn't want distance. Demi reached for his hand, and saw the bottle he was holding by the neck. He held it up for her inspection. A bottle of tequila, and a plastic bag with some limes swung from his fingers. "Hostess gift," he told her.

"Aw, you shouldn't have. Follow me. And I mean, literally, right behind me. I know where the cameras are, the directions they point, and the places that they miss."

"Got it. Lead the way, princess. Your dirty secret is safe with me."

Demi stopped and looked back. "What?" she said slowly. "What did you say?"

"You heard me," he replied.

"There is nothing dirty about this," she told him. "I'm not ashamed of what I'm doing. I have nothing to be ashamed of."

"Yeah? And all the complicated choreography?"

"My father remotely monitors the home security system with his tablet," she said. "He's obsessed about it. He gets a ping on his phone when the motion detectors are activated. He'll hear it, and he'll look."

"Ouch," he muttered. "That's dystopian as all fuck."

"Tell me about it," she said. "If he sees you here, they will turn around and drive back. Do you want to invite my parents to our encounter?"

They gazed at each other for a tense moment.

"Maybe we should call this off," she said. "If you're uncomfortable with being here, I totally understand. It is kind of weird. The sneaking, I mean. We can skip it."

He looked her up and down, and the hungry gleam in his eyes made her glad she'd taken off the bra, and chosen that skimpy, backless, draped gauze sundress. Her nipples hardened under his gaze, pressing against the thin fabric.

"No way," he said. "I'd sneak anywhere on earth for a taste of that."

Her knees went weak with relief. The rest of her tingled with anticipation. "Well okay, then. But it's not a dirty secret. By no means. It's just nobody else's goddamn business, for once in my goddamn life. Are we clear on that?"

"Crystal clear," he said.

"If I'd had more warning, I would have tried to find a way to get us out to the cabin on the lake," she said. "Spruce

Tip Island. That would have been perfect. There's no security out there. But we need a boat for that, and it's too complicated."

"Anywhere's fine," he said. "All I need is you."

The low growl of lust in his voice made her shiver, but she tried to play it cool. "So, you said in your text that you don't have to go to work tonight."

"That's right."

"That's awesome," she said. "We have until seven-thirty. That's when Granddad is dropping by to have coffee with me. And check up on me, of course."

"I'll be long gone by then," he assured her. "No worries."

She kept on standing there, trying to read his face. She couldn't put her finger on it. Something was different about him. Something had changed.

"What is it, Eric? What's going on?"

He frowned. "Nothing's wrong."

"I'm getting a strange vibe from you," she said. "I wish you'd tell me what's up."

He shook his head, but the silence kept getting heavier, charged with discomfort.

This was not okay. Demi clenched her jaw and just waited him out.

Finally, Eric shrugged. Angrily, as if he were shaking something off his back.

"Sorry," he said gruffly. "Some weird shit happened at work. It got me all uptight. I didn't mean to bring it here, but I guess I must have. It has nothing to do with you."

"I see. Do you want to talk about it?"

"No." His tone left no room for debate.

Now didn't seem like the moment to press him. It was

so new with them. Still just wild, sexy fantasy. Reality hadn't collided with it yet. She understood his desire to keep reality at arm's length, but that never worked. Not for long, anyway.

"Sorry," he said. "Let's get someplace private. I'll apologize so hard, I'll make your head spin."

"No need to apologize. Step only where I step, okay?"

She checked behind her to make sure he was following the torturous route that kept them out of camera and motion detector range. Then pushed open the door of the pool house open and turned on the light.

The pool house was connected with the garage, and Eric stopped for a moment to admire her dad's special toy, gleaming darkly in the shadows. The Porsche GT3 991.

Eric looked impressed. "Whoa," he murmured. "Sweet ride."

She gave the car an unfriendly glance. "Yeah, he loves that thing. You'd have thought he'd use it for the road trip with my mom, right? What with the gorgeous weather and the beautiful mountain roads? Mom loves riding in it. But no. It's Dad's bad boy car, and she doesn't fit that picture for him. He drives his Volvo station wagon when he's with Mom."

Eric's eyes narrowed. "I see," he said. "Bitter much?"

"I guess so. Sorry. That's my version of the weird shit that we won't talk about tonight. Like your thing at work. My parents' issues don't get any air time."

"Tonight's just for us," he said. "Fuck all the rest of it."

"My thoughts exactly." She switched off the light and led him into the kitchen.

He turned around, taking it all in. "You could feed an army with this kitchen."

"My mom did a lot of entertaining when I was a kid," she said. "Not so much anymore. I grew up watching her set a buffet for sixty people like it was nothing. It's one of the things that got me interested in cooking. Speaking of which." She gestured toward the fridge. "I could make you a drink. Are you thirsty, or hungry, or—"

"For you."

She cut off her hostess blather and laughed. "Okay. That's fine, too."

"You really think you can shimmy around in front of me in a backless dress with no bra and then offer me cookies and tea?"

She shrugged. "I was thinking more in terms of a sandwich and a beer."

"No," he said. "Just get me a couple of shot glasses and some salt. And a plate for the lime." He took a knife from the knife-block on the island and sliced one into wedges.

"Shots?" she said. "Already? The evening is young."

"I'm calling the vibe tonight. And it's not going to be cookies and tea."

Her hands shook with delicious nervousness as she set out two shot glasses and a plate and poured a little salt into saucer. He still seemed different today.

As dangerously sexy as always, but with more emphasis on the danger.

Maybe it was what had happened at work. Maybe it was just the Vaughan house, working its twisted bad magic on him. Maybe it had been a mistake to invite him here. Having him in her family's home underscored the differences between their backgrounds. It unleashed complicated feelings that neither one of them was ready to deal with.

This dark, angry energy from him was unsettling. Still arousing, though. But everything about him aroused her. Even the way he poured the tequila into shot glasses.

"So, ah..." She tried to keep her voice steady. "Tour of the house?"

"Yeah, if it's straight to your bedroom with no detours." He put the pinch of salt on his hand, licked it off, tossed back his shot glass and bit the lime. Then he took her hand, kissed it and put salt on it. He held up her glass.

"Lick it off," he said softly.

The command felt erotic, almost dirty. Cascades of images of the waterfall pool and what he'd done to her there rushed through her mind. What they'd done in the car.

She licked the salt. Drank the shot. Bit the lime. Salty, bitter, sour. Then he seized her, dragging her into a ravenous kiss. So incredibly hot and sweet. It melted her.

She lost herself in it, arching and moaning. The shot glass fell from her hand.

Eric snagged it in mid-air without even looking. "I'll hang onto this for later," he said. "Your room. Lead the way."

"Okay." Her voice was quavering.

She noticed the phenomenon again as she led him through the various rooms of the house. He moved so silently. In spite of the cracking, popping and creaking floorboards in the aged Victorian mansion, in spite of his size, his feet made no sound.

But she didn't need to hear him to know that he was back there.

His sexual energy pressed against her like heat from a raging bonfire.

# 12

Eric focused on Demi's stunning ass as she went up the stairs in front of him. The sway of her hips and that sexy rounded shape was fucking hypnotizing. Her skimpy dress was almost sheer, and was backless, scooping down almost to the cleft of her ass cheeks.

A beautiful expanse of smooth, perfect tanned skin.

And he was about to touch it. Every inch of her, he would touch and kiss and lick.

She left a trail of her own sweet scent wafting behind her. He tried to breathe every last molecule, hating to waste it. The fuzzy ringlets of her freshly-washed, scented hair bounced and swung over the dips and curves of her tanned back.

There was a little triangle of moles on her left shoulder-blade. Her skin was so fine textured. Amazingly smooth. Just that bikini strap band right across her back, of creamy paleness. Her shoulder-blades were delicate. Her spine elegantly curved.

His hands burned to touch and handle every flare and

dip and swell and shadow. Delve inside all the tender inside places. He wanted to know it all. Claim it all.

*Cool it. Don't get ahead of yourself. Breathe and wait.*

He focused on Demi, since the dollhouse-like perfection of their home bothered him. All the expensive antique furniture, ceramics and art. Puffy brocade chairs and couches. Persian rugs, hardwood floors, molded tin ceilings, fancy woodwork, stained glass insets. It was like being in a fucking jewel box.

It was safer just to look at her. He made an exception for the photos on the stairway. They were mostly of Demi at various times in her life, and she'd been beautiful since babyhood. No surprise there. Those amazing eyes.

Once upstairs, she led him down to the end of the upstairs corridor and into a large bedroom, which was pretty much like what he'd expected. Old-fashioned, super-girly. A wooden four-poster with a frilly lace canopy and coverlet. A heap of piled up decorative pillows. An old-time doll with a frilly bonnet over her brown curls sat right in the middle propped against a pillow. She stared at him balefully with round, glassy blue eyes.

Demi made a sound of annoyance and laid down the salt and limes on her dresser before snatching up the doll and stowing her on a shelf.

"My mom keeps putting her back on the bed," she said. "Plus all these damn pillows. A freaking mountain of them, every time my back is turned. I'm always knocking them off and tripping over them."

"It's fine." He was amused at her embarrassment. "Doesn't bother me."

"It bothers me," she said heatedly. "I feel like I'm stuck in a nineteenth century novel. And there's the privacy thing.

But whatever. Her house, her rules. It's only a few more weeks."

Eric set the tequila down on a white-painted vanity that was crowded with make-up and perfume bottles. "I'll drink to that. Give me your hand."

He poured out their shots, stopping to suck tenderly on her fingertips until she was gasping for breath. He finally anointed their hands with salt and held up her shot glass.

"To freedom," he said.

"God, yes." She took it, and drank. "Whew," she sputtered. "Strong."

Eric took the shot glass from her hands, set it on the vanity and faced her.

*Breathe and wait.* He just held her gaze and let the silence build.

Demi had been about to speak, but it looked as if she'd forgotten what she wanted to say. She gazed back at him, eyes wide. Lips parted. Breathing fast.

She swayed toward him, opening the dance.

He hooked the thin shoulder straps of her dress in his fingers. Barely a tug made them fall. The neckline caught on her taut nipples.

A twitch of his fingers freed it and the bodice fell to her waist. Ahhh.

He'd seen her naked. He'd touched and kissed and licked and fucked her, but her beauty poleaxed him all over again. It always reduced him to a stammering, slack-jawed beginner. His smooth technique went straight to hell. Every damn time.

It was like she was lit up from the inside. She glowed like a star. Her nipples were so tight and dark against the creamy skin of her breasts.

He cupped them reverently. The contact put his fingertips into a state of shock all their own. So flower-petal soft. Springy and yielding. She shuddered and moaned.

He gestured at the bench in front of the vanity. "You think that will hold us both?"

"No idea. It's never been tested."

"We're about to find out. I like the mirror. I want to look at you from every angle at once." He pulled the bench out farther and straddled it, with a leg on either side, facing the mirror. He held out his hand. "Mount up."

Demi licked her full bottom lip, hitched up her skirt and swung her tanned, shapely leg over his, setting her warm, soft weight right against the bulge of his erection. Her gorgeous bare breasts, full and soft, were right in his face.

That was a surefire way to take his mind off his problems. Nothing could occupy his mind while Demi's nipple was in his mouth, her pussy pressing his aching erection.

He caressed her with his mouth, nuzzling and licking and sucking. Deep, slow, caressing pulls. She moved against him, wrapping her arms around his neck. He felt her breath shuddering and catching in her lungs as she rode him, rising and falling. Wiggling and writhing. Rubbing her melting heat against his aching hardness. Slowly…slowly.

He could do this forever. Rocking, heaving, holding her, suckling her…

She threw her head back and went rigid in his arms as her first orgasm wrenched through her. He almost came in his pants as he felt the pleasure pulsate through her body.

But he held back. Rode it out. Not yet. He eased himself back from the danger zone, eyes squeezed shut as he slowly…breathed…it…down. *Save it, goddamnit.*

"Oh, God," she whispered. "Eric. That was so good."

"I'll drink to that. No, don't move. I'll do it from here."

Demi steadied herself by clutching his shoulders as he reached around her to pour the shots. He committed every detail of her to memory while he set her up with the salt and the lime. The drops of moisture beading her hairline, the way her throat moved when she drank. The gleam of moisture on her lips after she bit into the lime, gasping and laughing at the intense tastes. Her pink tongue licking away salt crystals and tangy lime juice.

The evening sunshine coming in her window lit up her hair. It glowed like a halo.

He set his glass back down and seized her. Kissed her like he was afraid she would be snatched away. But tonight was no time for doubts or fears. His or hers.

Tonight, he'd keep her busy like a runaway train. Too busy to worry or wonder.

*Crack.*

Eric was already on his feet, cupping her ass. Holding her up as he kicked away the bench that had given way beneath them. A leg had snapped off.

"Fuck," he muttered. "We broke your bench. Sorry."

"Oops," she murmured, her thighs tightening around him, arms winding around his neck. "It's okay. Look at you, Eric. Those are some serious reflexes you've got there."

"I guess. I'll take a look at it after. Fix it for you before your folks come back."

"Let's worry about that later."

"Fair enough." He kicked the bench away and turned her to face the mirror, setting her back down on her feet. He clamped her against his body. He tugged her skirt up until it was barely more than a sash of twisted fabric around her waist. Beneath it, she wore a burgundy lace thong. He kissed her neck. "Lose the panties," he murmured into her ear.

The heat inside him jacked up still higher as her panties dropped around her ankles. He admired the bikini tan line on her hip, the paleness around the swatch of pussy hair.

"Demi," he said thickly. "You're perfect."

"Ah…thanks." She licked her lips. "You're hot yourself. You're burning me up."

"I have barely begun to burn you up. Put your foot up on the vanity."

She gave him a puzzled look but obliged, perching her foot against the vanity. Her toenails were painted a pale color that caught the light like mother of pearl.

He seized her knee with his hand and pulled her leg out, opening her wide. "Show me," he said. "I want to see your pussy. It's so beautiful."

She laughed, embarrassed. "Well, there I am. Look your fill."

And that was it for coherent words. The sight of her all open to him rendered him non-verbal. He just stared, feeling the crazy triple-time drum of his heartbeat.

Her pussy was all different shades of shining hot pink, furled up like the petals of a tropical orchid. The darker inner lips poking out, flushed and gleaming.

Look your fill, hah. Like he could ever get enough. In a lifetime.

Eric pressed his mouth to the side of her neck, kissing and nuzzling while he reached down to worship her with his hands. One delicately working her clit, the other stroking her pussy lips. Easing his finger into hot, clinging perfection.

He could have petted her for hours. She barely lasted for a couple of minutes before she went taut in his arms, crying out. Her pussy gripped his fingers as rhythmic pulsations of pleasure shuddered through her.

They echoed through him. It felt almost as if he was coming along with her. He loved it. His pulsing erection pressed against her ass, desperate for action.

"I was going to pour a shot whenever you came," he murmured into her ear. "But you're on a hair trigger tonight. We have to pace ourselves."

"How about when you come? Let's drink to that."

"In good time. I want you primed. I want it to be so fucking good for you."

"It already is." She turned around, reaching for the buttons on his jeans. "And it's about to get better. Let's get these off you."

He dropped the jeans, and Demi made a low, pleased sound in her throat as his stiff penis rose up into her hand. Hot and hard and eager for her touch. "Oh, Eric," she whispered, squeezing and stroking. "You're gorgeous."

He kicked off his sandals and pulled her dress down until it dropped to the carpet.

"That's better," he said, turning her to face the mirror again. He couldn't stop dividing his passionate admiration between the front view and the back. He wanted to touch everything at once.

Their eyes locked in the mirror. Demi smiled at him, and shifted her weight. She bent forward, placing her hand against the vanity. Widening her legs, arching her back.

Her hair slid over her bare shoulders as she turned to look back at him. Lips curved in a sultry smile of invitation.

Eric dug into the bag he'd brought with him for the condoms with hands that shook. He sheathed himself in record time and positioned himself behind her. Stroking her ass cheeks. Petting her pussy lips first with his fingertips, then with his dick.

He slid it up and down her labia, spreading her slippery lube all around to ease his way. Drawing back when she pushed back against him.

Not yet. No rush.

"Goddamnit, Eric," she said, breathless and impatient. "What are you waiting for?"

"Not waiting. Just enjoying the moment. I like petting you with my dick…just like this. Does that feel good?"

Shudders of pleasure racked her. "You're playing power games."

"Maybe," he admitted. "Whatever makes you hot. Whatever makes you wet. Whatever makes you come. That's what I'll do. Count on it." He reached around her, taking her clit in the cleft between his fingers, squeezing it tenderly as he eased the end of his penis slowly inside.

She jerked, gasping. Her pussy muscles fluttering around his cockhead, hugging him.

"Eric," she whispered, shakily. "Please."

His control snapped. He made a harsh sound in his throat and drove inside her.

# 13

She cried out at the delicious invasion. Surging deep, sliding out. Slow, deliberate thrusts. Each one made her softer, took him deeper.

Like every time, she was taken over by a wild energy. Possessed by desire that sprang up from someplace deep inside herself. A place that was newly discovered. Every time, she got a startling glimpse of something huge, infinite, magnificent. Unknown.

She heard sounds, and realized that she was the one making them. The stuff on her vanity was rattling in tempo. Makeup tubes, lotion bottles, jolting to the rhythms of his thrusts. Perfume bottles and lipsticks tumbled and rolled. Some hit the carpet.

The dance of their bodies was all that existed, the skillful thrust and swivel and glide of his penis inside her. He kept the pace relentlessly slow, controlling it utterly. His hands gripped her hips. Every maddening, pumping stroke primed her for the next.

He drove her to a yelling, writhing frenzy before he

relented, and fucked her harder, with all the intensity they both craved. Driving her over the top.

Her climax was huge, wrenching and sweet. Pulsing ripples of delicious warmth that felt endless. After, a shimmering glow like moonlight on water. So sweet.

She met his eyes in the mirror sometime later when she became conscious that he was still inside her. Motionless. Still completely erect. "You didn't come?"

He slid out of her, shaking his head, then pulled her body upright, close against his. He gently bit her shoulder, then licked it. "I'm saving it," he said softly in her ear.

He had the faraway look in his eyes again. She didn't like it.

"You're playing games with me," she told him.

"Am I?" His smile flashed. "Tell me all about it."

"The lofty sex god from on high. Making me come over and over, but never giving up your own self-control. I love your self-control, don't get me wrong. You're amazing. But I want to see you lose it. I want to see you explode."

He was silent for a moment, nuzzling her hair. "It's not so simple," he said. "I've never felt like this before with anyone. I have to fight to stay on top of myself. I don't want to hurt you or scare you. I'm not holding back to spite you."

"You won't hurt me or scare me. Stop fighting so hard. I want to know you."

For a moment, she felt embarrassed. Like a spoiled child demanding a treat. Who the hell was she to insist on knowing him? She didn't even know herself. She'd learned more about Demi Vaughan in the last twenty-four hours with Eric than she'd ever known about herself before that.

But now wasn't a good moment to back down.

So she went to the bed and batted off the excess

pillows. Turned down the bedcover and sheet and draped herself across it in a seductive pose. She spread her hair artfully over the pillow and tilted her breasts up, magazine centerfold style.

She gave him a sultry glance. "So? What now?" she asked in a throaty voice. "You shameless tease."

"You think?" Eric climbed onto the bed, gripping his erection at the base so it jutted aggressively. "I'm taking you at your word." His voice had a warning tone.

"I'd expect nothing less of you."

Eric seized her knee, folded modestly over, and spread it wide. He stared down between her legs, then laid his hand over her mound. "Mine." His voice was steely.

She was startled. "What? What's yours?"

"This." He stroked her pussy lips, and tenderly thrust his finger inside.

She felt herself clench around him, and lifted herself to his caressing hand.

"Wow," she whispered shakily. "Ah…that's possessive."

"Yes," he agreed. "It is. Very."

She looked at him for a long, blank moment before a coherent reply formed in her mind. "It's a bit premature, making ownership claims about my body."

"I know that. I never said that it was true. Or that it was right. I know you belong to yourself. But that's how touching your pussy makes me feel. Isn't that what you wanted to know? How I feel?"

She hesitated. "Ah…yes."

"Well, there you go. Touching your pussy makes me possessive." His voice was rough. "When it's all sweet and soft and hot and ready for me to fuck, this huge animal thing roars up, and that's what it says. That's all it says. Mine. Mine. Mine."

He lifted up her mound delicately, parting her pussy lips, making her clit pop out.

"So I try to control myself," he murmured. "To stay out of trouble."

She choked off a moan as he bent down and circled his tongue around her clit. Lapping it, licking it, loving it. "Oh my God, Eric. Please."

"Mine to suck and lick and tongue-fuck." He slid his tongue tenderly inside her opening. "You taste so good. That sweet juice. That's all mine, too. I want to lick it up."

His deep voice vibrating against her mound made her crazy. She reached down, winding her fingers into his hair and tugging. "I wanted to make it about you for once," she protested. "If we're going to do oral sex, let me drive you crazy for a change."

He rolled between her splayed legs. "I thought you wanted to know my secrets."

"I do, but— "

"Number one, I'm possessive. Number two, I suck at taking orders."

"Ah, yes. I did notice that already." She arched back as he stroked her clit with the head of his cock. Around…and around, making soft, juicy sounds as it moved inside her.

"Number three," he went on. "I like to be in charge."

She stared up, breath jerking between her parted lips as he prodded his cockhead inside her. "Yeah? Then we might have a problem. I like being in charge, too."

"Yeah? How do you like…*this?*" He thrust forward, driving inside her.

She came almost immediately. Her pussy clutching him

hard.

When her eyes fluttered open, Eric was watching her, looking pleased with himself. "I don't think we're going to have any problems," he murmured.

She writhed eagerly against his deep, driving thrusts, surrendering to pleasure. Driven to the edge of madness by his expert fucking—and then beyond it.

They exploded together.

It was a long time before she moved at all. She was limp, drenched with sweat.

She opened her eyes and found that her leg was splayed over his thigh, his penis still inside her. It was only slightly softer than usual.

She wiggled against him. "I take it you came this time, at least? It felt like you did."

He cupped her ass with his hand, pulling to stay inside her. "Yeah."

"Good," she murmured. "But you're still hard."

"You just have that effect on me. I have to get rid of this condom, whatever we decide to do about my hard-on." He pulled out, with a sigh of regret. "Mmm, you feel good. So where do I…?"

"Bathroom's through that door," she said, pointing.

She admired his tight, muscular ass as he went into the bathroom. The water started running. The sky was fading to a deeper blue now. One bright star glowed through the window, low on the horizon.

The door opened. Eric stood silhouetted in the doorway before switching the light back off. He came back to the bed, pulled out another condom and rolled it on with the matter-of-fact attitude of a guy who was absolutely in charge.

"Already?" she said.

"We can rest, if you want. I just want to be ready in case I get lucky again. No rush. My hard-on isn't going anywhere. It's your call, Demi. Always."

Demi blew out a shaky breath, rolled away from him and got up. She needed a breather. Over-the-top charisma, mind-melting sexual mojo, the unwavering self-possession, it was just too much. She could hardly breathe.

She fled to the bathroom to collect herself. Once there, she washed up and stared at her face, barely recognizing herself in the mirror. She looked dazed, soft. Face and chest hot pink. Hair a wild, tousled mane. Lips puffy and red from all the passionate kissing.

She'd never felt that close to anyone. Not even herself. This was completely out of hand. Her guard hadn't just fallen. It was entirely gone. She was naked, and madly in love.

On a fucking epic scale. A soul-crushing, world-ending, Greek tragedy scale, if it didn't work out. And the statistical probabilities of it working out…well.

They were not great.

# 14

Eric waited for Demi to get out the bathroom, wondering if he'd fucked up again.

She was taking her time in there. Too much time.

After a half hour had passed, he concluded that he'd done it again. True to form, he'd overdone it. Come down on her like a ton of bricks. She'd panicked.

*Fuck.*

After the never-ending shower, she finally emerged, wrapped in a towel and a cloud of scented steam. His clueless dick sprang up to full attention. Hello, sex maniac. He should have gotten into bed and rolled onto his belly. Given her a breather from that constant visual reminder of how crazy he was for her.

"Hey," he said.

Her gaze flicked down to his stiff, empurpled penis, then back up to his face.

He gave her a 'what-of-it' shrug. "You okay? You were in there for a long time."

"I'm fine," she said. "Just needed a moment to think."

"What about?"

She shook her head. "I just can't have a calm, rational conversation with that enormous hard-on waving in the air between us. It's distracting."

He reached for his jeans, crestfallen. "I'll get dressed."

"No you most certainly will not," she said crisply. "Drop those right now, Eric Trask."

The jeans flopped to the ground. "No?" He hoped he did not look and sound as pathetically hopeful as he felt in that moment.

"We're not there yet. We still have until seven-thirty, when Granddad gets here. Call it seven, to be safe."

Oh thank God. He scooted to the other side of the bed, draping the sheet over his relentless hard-on. "Great. Dick under wraps. Problem solved. Come here and let's talk about whatever's bugging you."

She sat down on the bed and curled her legs up, keeping the towel wrapped around herself. "I was thinking about what you said before. How you like being in charge."

"Aw, shit," he said. "Pay no attention to that. I was just talking dirty, to get you all worked up. It was all in the interests of making you come. Don't worry about it."

"Let me finish," she said sternly. "There are a few things that need to be said up front. You know. Ground rules."

He flopped back against the pillow. "Okay, go ahead," he said. "Hit me."

"For one thing, I don't believe for one second that you were just talking dirty to turn me on. I know blather when I hear it, and that wasn't blather. You were telling me the truth. At least the truth about how you felt in that moment."

"Fine," he said. "Guilty as charged. I did not lie. And?

So?"

"So it's a problem," she said. "You're going to be constantly frustrated with me."

He rolled onto his side, the better to study the curve of her cheekbone. The worried look in her big eyes, full of shadows. "Why would that be?"

"I'm not going to let anybody be in charge of me." Her voice was resolute. "Because I'm sick of that. A new era is dawning in my life."

"Great," he said. "You're a woman on a mission. With her own agenda. Super-hot. I love it. It works for me."

"I'm difficult and bullheaded," she went on. "Just ask my parents."

He gave her a cautious, sidewise look. "Uh…"

"On second thought, don't. Just take my word for it."

"That sounds safer," he agreed.

"I've got plans, and I won't compromise them. For anything or anyone."

"Check, check and check," he said. "I've got plans, too. We'll both be busy as hell doing challenging things. Sounds stimulating. Still not seeing the problem here."

She stared searchingly into his face, a frown between her brows. "I didn't want you going off on some overheated fantasy about being the boss. That's not happening."

It took a supreme act of will, but he knew laughing would fuck him up. He groped for the words to set them back onto the straight and narrow path toward redemption.

"I wouldn't dare try that," he said. "I boss myself, and you'll do the same. It'll work out fine. We might have sparks fly here and there, but it won't get boring."

Her eyes narrowed. "What's that supposed to mean?"

Eric went on, warming to his topic. "The drama will

play out in bed, every night," he said. "I'll use all my sexual sorcery to try to bend you to my wicked will. But it won't work, because you're so fucking indomitable. You'll just put me in my place. Over and over and over. Until we're so hot and sweaty and exhausted we can barely roll over. Oh, man. I am up for that." He lifted the sheet, glancing down at himself. "Literally."

She gave him a narrow look. "Are you messing with me? Because I'm serious."

"I don't have a death wish." He kept his face solemn. "You are the queen of yourself and I respect your sovereignty."

"Now you're being a smart-ass."

He lifted the covers, beckoning to her. "I didn't mean to be. Cross my heart. Lose the towel and come over here to me. Please. Just to cuddle."

She let the towel fall to the floor, and slid in next to him.

*Whoa.* He practically had an instant whole body orgasm from the sweet warm rush of skin-on-skin contact. Slender arms, shapely legs, silken flower-scented hair. That baby-smooth skin, as soft as a cloud.

All his senses went nuts. He could pound nails with his dick, but he wasn't going to. He just edged as close as he dared, stroking her gently from shoulder to thigh.

He didn't dare kiss her, or he'd end up fucking her again. Didn't even look at her. He tucked her head under his chin and kept his eyes closed. Iron control.

After a while, the soft blooming heat of her breath against his bare chest got slower and more even. She'd dozed off.

He couldn't resist watching at her sleeping face. So

beautiful, it hurt to look.

Caring that much. So fucking dangerous. It was begging to get slammed. He'd known that for a long time, even before the GodsAcre fire. He'd known it since Mom died. He stroked a lock of Demi's hair, marveling at the miraculous texture of it.

Precious, fragile things, like love. So delicate. Easy to fuck up. Easy to destroy.

But he didn't have a choice. Demi had torn his heart wide open. He couldn't keep her out. The damage was done. There was no going back.

All he could do was brace himself for the pain.

---

Demi woke up to moonlight flooding through her windows. She was wrapped in warmth, and Eric was gazing at her, stroking her hair.

"Hey," she murmured. "Can't sleep?"

He shook his head. "I don't want to miss a second of this feeling," he said.

She nestled closer, smiling. "What feeling?"

His arms tightened. "Like I could do anything," he said. "Move mountains. Fly to the moon. Any fucking thing I could imagine."

"Me, too." She reached out to caress his face with wondering fingers. Feeling the fine rasp of his beard shadow, the hot, damp skin. His beautiful bone structure. She peered down at his body. He was still fiercely erect. And he already had a condom on. That was handy.

She reached down and seized his rod, stroking him gently.

His hands covered hers. "Demi, you don't have to—"

"I know I don't," she said. "We've been through that. I'm the queen of myself, remember?"

"But we've had sex twice already."

"How fortunate for you that you manage to keep up with my voracious sexual desires," she told him.

Eric's laugher choked off into a moan as she stroked her hand down to the base of his shaft, squeezing him boldly and making sure the condom was in place.

"Oh, God, Demi," he rasped. "Please."

"Yes," she replied, tugging at his shoulders.

Eric followed her cues, rolling carefully over on top of her, and rested his weight on his elbows. Then he leaned over to flip on the bedside light. It produced a mellow, orangey glow. "I need to see you," he said. "You're so damn beautiful. I have to stare."

God, he was gorgeous. All the defined contours of his big, heavily muscled body poised over hers, set off by stark shadows and soft light, it was overwhelming. She could feel her own heart beating heavily, in her chest, in her lips. Between her legs.

She shifted beneath him, reaching down to grip his dick, rubbing it wantonly against herself. Making him wet with her lube, then nudging him inside. Wiggling and straining to get closer. Take him deeper.

Eric rocked forward, pushing himself inside her. "Tell me when it's too much," he said. "I could go on forever."

"I'm good," she said. "Don't worry. I want forever, too."

They both froze for a breathless instant as her words sank in. Eric's eyes flashed, but he made no comment. He just bent down, kissing her with tender intensity. "I'll keep going until you tell me to stop."

"Bold words," she said.

"I'm nothing if not bold. Look at me the whole time. I go for that."

As if she could look away. Eric Trask, arched over her body, pumping his body into her. Every thrust making her gasp. Unraveling her with pleasure.

His gaze was fierce and relentless. She understood the message of his body, with every deep, gliding stroke of his cock. *Mine. Mine. Mine.*

He didn't need to ask if it was good for her. He knew. He was fused with her.

Pleasure overwhelmed them together. Swept them both away.

They lay together, still joined, for a timeless interval afterward. Eric reluctantly pulled away from her, to her sleepy protests, and went to deal with the condom. He was back in a matter of seconds, wrapping his hot, naked body around hers once again.

She'd never felt so perfectly happy as she did in that moment. Floating in daydreams. Hunting for an apartment with him in Seattle. With the big city rents, they'd probably have to share a studio apartment for a while. It would be tight, in all senses.

And so much fun. Freaking delicious. It made her high just thinking of it.

The sound of a car motor and headlights flickering in the trees jolted Demi out of her reverie. It sent her bounding up into the air like a spring.

"Holy shit," she said, panicked. "They came back early. Oh, shit, shit, *shit!*"

"Demi," Eric said gently. "Chill."

"Do not tell me to chill!" She snatched up his pants and

flung them at his chest. "Get dressed! Quick! If we're quick, you can slip out pool house door before he—"

"No."

"What do you mean, no?" she yelled. "Move, damn it! Do you have a death wish?"

Eric got out of the bed. "I'll get dressed," he said, stepping into his jeans. "But I'm not running out of here like a rabbit. If he's come back, that means he saw me on the security cameras. So why the frenzy? We're busted. Grit your teeth. We'll get through it."

"I just want to spare you what I promise will be some of the shittiest moments of your life!"

Eric let out a short laugh as he stepped into his sandals and wrestled his T-shirt on. "Sorry, babe, but nothing Ben Vaughan can throw at me could even begin to touch the shittiest moments of my life," he said. "I'm not afraid of him. But I'm sorry that you are."

"You really want to be insulted and abused? Why would you do that to yourself?"

"I don't like to back down," he told her.

"I don't want to do this, Eric! Not tonight!"

"Then you shouldn't have invited me here. If you can't do the time, don't do the crime."

She looked shocked. "Are you for real? You are muscling me into this showdown with my dad whether I like it or not?"

"Yes," he said. "Are we together, Demi? Or not?"

"That's not the point! Don't be an idiot!"

"It's the only point," he said. "Answer my question. Are we together? It's your call. I'm on board if you are." He waited. "So? Let's hear it."

She looked wildly back from the flickering light outside

to his face. The car stopped. Then the engine went into reverse.

There was a crashing, clattering sound. Demi lunged at the window.

Eric came up behind her and looked over her shoulder. There was a big silver Jeep in the turnaround, backing away from the barbeque on the patio, which had been knocked over. It lurched over a bed of petunias, knocked over a bird bath, and bumped, slowly and unsteadily, over a low border of shrubbery and back up onto the driveway.

It accelerated away. Not her father's Volvo station wagon.

"That's not my parents." Her voice was thin. "That's Burt Colby. The guy who knocked over the mailbox. He's drunk again. Must have pulled in here by mistake."

She winced at the faint crashing sound. "Ouch. There goes the mailbox again."

They both watched the flicker of headlights as Burt Colby extricated his car from the bushes at the end of the driveway, pulled onto the main road and lurched onward.

Demi put her hands over her hot cheeks, willing her heart to slow down. "Shit," she whispered again.

Eric stepped back, saying nothing. The silence was deafening.

Demi grabbed her robe off the hook on the bathroom door. She shrugged it over her naked body and tied the sash with sharp, angry gestures. "Well," she said. "That was a buzzkill."

"Pretty much," he agreed.

"Sorry about the false alarm."

"I wasn't alarmed," Eric said. "I was perfectly ready for them. Bring 'em on. But you never answered my question. Are we together? Or not?"

She flung her hair back, making an impatient sound. "Eric, you're stressing me out. Now is not the time for this particular conversation."

"So by not answering me, you're answering me, right?"

"Don't throw an ultimatum in my face," she snapped. "I get plenty of that from my dad, and I don't need any more from you."

He let out a slow, careful breath. "Okay. I guess that's my cue."

"What's that supposed to mean? What cue?"

"To slink back into the hole in the wall that I came out of. Preferably without being seen by anyone respectable. Until stud services are required of me again."

She recoiled. "Stud services…? You son of a bitch!"

"Just calling it what it is," he said. "It's too bad we were interrupted. I could have given you the classic dirty secret treatment. Fucked you all over the house. We'd leave red-hot, carnal memories in every room. I could give you head on the dining room table, pound you from behind while bending you over the Porsche in the garage. You could blow me while I sit in the desk chair in the study—"

"You asshole!"

"This is a big house," he went on. "I might have to do it in two shifts. Then again, you make me rock-hard, so maybe we could cover the whole place in a single night."

She slapped his face, then stared at her stinging hand, horrified at the sudden change between them. She'd gone from being so happy, so high. From looking down on the whole world, feeling sorry for everyone who wasn't the two of them…to this.

Everything her father touched turned ugly. Now he'd

managed to taint this, too, somehow. Without even making a big entrance.

From heaven to hell in a single blink.

Eric touched the red mark on his cheek. "I guess I deserved that," he said, after a moment. "I was out of line."

"Just leave. Right now." Her lips felt numb.

Eric looked around the ravaged room. The broken bench, the sheets half pulled off the bed, the vanity dragged away from the wall, makeup and bottles scattered on the floor, the condom wrappers, the shot glasses, the wedges of lime and spilled salt everywhere.

"This place looks like it got chewed up by a tornado," he said. "Can I help clean up? I could fix the bench, at least. Carry away the evidence."

"No thank you, I'll handle it," she said. "I said to get…*out.*" She shoved at him, but as before, it was like pushing on the trunk of an enormous tree. No give.

Eric grabbed the tequila bottle by the neck and walked out into the corridor.

She followed him out. He turned at the bottom of the stairs to look up at her.

"Yesterday, you said it was too soon to ask you to run away with me," he said. "You said we should wait until we've had our first fight."

Demi wiped tears off your face. "What are you talking about?"

"We had our first fight," he said. "And it was a real motherfucker."

"You could say that."

"It's stupid to say this when you're so mad at me, but I still want to run away with you. I told you that I love you, and I meant it. I just want that to be clear."

The nerve of him staggered her. "Fuck off, Eric."

He just stood there, gazing up at her with that bleak, faraway look in his eyes.

"You talk a good game," he said quietly. "You act all rebellious and tough, but it's just an act. You're just a scared little girl shaking in your shoes. Under Daddy's thumb."

"Get out of this house, Eric."

"What we have is special," he continued, relentless. "But it comes at a price. If you ever decide to grow a pair, give me a call."

"Don't hold your breath."

He nodded. "Understood. Goodbye, Demi." He disappeared through the kitchen entryway. She heard the door open, then heard it snick shut behind him.

Demi's legs gave out. She sank down onto the stairs and burst into tears.

# 15

Eric didn't bother with all of Demi's convoluted choreography for avoiding the security cameras once he was back outside. Fuck that. He was done slinking around.

Sure enough, the mailbox was knocked over again. This time it lay flat on the ground, but he didn't bother hoisting it back into position. It didn't seem appropriate this time.

He got to his car and found all four of the Monster's tires slashed. Flat to the ground.

A fresh disaster, in his broke-ass state. He had no money for a tow. He'd have to walk down from the Heights, all the way through town, and then out to Otis's. Over ten miles in all. Then he had to beg Anton or Otis to help him drag his piece-of-shit car home until he found a solution. Any funds that might have gone toward fixing the damage were frozen in the form of a boulder opal and diamond engagement ring.

Destined for a woman who'd just told him to fuck off.

He deserved it, pissing and moaning like a foul-mouthed little bitch. Jeremiah would have knocked his ass into next week if he heard Eric mouthing off to a lady like that. The Prophet had entertained antique, old-timey notions about women, but he had believed in being polite, protective and respectful of them.

With a few notable exceptions. Like, getting Mom a timely course of antibiotics for her cough during that last winter up at GodsAcre. Like remembering that fifteen-year-old Fiona was a person, not a thing be traded to some sleazy asshole for services rendered.

The respecting and protecting part had broken down, in the end. Along with Jeremiah's sanity.

That was the fucking Prophet's Curse for you. Maybe he, too, was programmed to destroy what he loved. Maybe Demi would have a healthier, happier life if she stayed far away from him and his fucking family curse.

*Shut up, Trask. You're whining again. Boo-hoo, poor fucking you.*

He took off, walking fast. Disgusted at himself, he hadn't gone more than a half a mile before he heard a car motor rumbling behind him, and the flicker of headlights in the dim glow of dawn. He shifted to the side of the road to let it go by, and was surprised and mildly alarmed to see the car slow as it passed, then pull to an abrupt stop.

Alarm bells went off. Holy shit. For real? Another Porsche GT3 991. Black, just like the one in Demi's dad's garage. What were the odds of seeing two of those in the space of a few hours? He walked toward the idling car, and saw Boyd Nevins at the wheel.

Boyd leaned toward him with a weirdly friendly smile. The window hummed down. "Hey. Eric? That you?"

Eric stared at him. It made no sense. Boyd's family was

by no means poor, but they didn't have Porsche GT3 kind of money. And it was even more strange that Boyd would speak to Eric at all, considering what a dickhead he'd been to all three of the Trask brothers during their stint at Shaw's Crossing High School.

"You're out early," Boyd said.

"So are you," Eric observed.

"What brings you out here at four-thirty in the morning?"

"Car trouble," Eric said.

"No surprise, with that rolling turd that you drive. Need a lift?"

Eric gazed at him, perplexed. "Why the fuck would you offer me a ride?"

Boyd gave him that manic grin again. "Look, man. Sure, I was a tool to you and your brothers back in high school, but that was years ago, okay? I'm not that guy anymore. Live and learn. Everybody grows, you get me?"

Eric just stared at him, unconvinced. Boyd had never struck him as big on growth.

"You need to get out to Otis's," Boyd said. "That's Vensel Road, right? For a shot of that tequila, I'll give you a ride to the crossroads. That'll save you six miles at least."

Eric glanced down at the bottle in his hand. It occurred to him that he didn't want to drink that tequila. He handed the bottle through the window to Boyd. Good riddance.

"Thanks, man." Boyd popped out the cork and took a generous swig.

"You drink while you drive this thing?" Eric observed. "Not smart."

Boyd laughed a little too loud. "Oh, c'mon. One sip. Stop lecturing me like a fucking Sunday school teacher and get in the damn car."

Eric looked at Boyd, then back up toward Demi's house. He wanted the Monster away from the Vaughan home as soon as possible, but if he was on foot, it would take over two hours just to get home. Add to that however long it took for him to enlist Otis, Anton or Mace's assistance.

Demi's folks would be back by then for sure. He didn't know if he and Demi had a chance in hell of being together after pissing her off as badly as he just had. If they did, maybe there was some sense in standing his ground.

But if they didn't, he had no business leaving his crap car right next to her house for her folks to freak out about. Making needless trouble for her.

Fuck. He had to get moving before he made things worse for everyone.

He pulled open the door of the Porsche and got in. "Thanks, man. Appreciate it."

"No problem," Boyd said.

The car took off with a screech. The smell of the car's luxe interior surrounded him. Spotless cream colored leather. Boyd flung his head back, swigging tequila.

"Dude," Eric said. "Go easy on that. Give me the bottle. I'll hold it for you."

"Don't sweat it." Boyd stuck the bottle between his legs as the car picked up still more speed, squealing around the sharp curve at the bottom of the Heights and peeling out onto the main drag toward the heart of downtown Shaw's Crossing. "One more favor, man. Can I use your phone? I need to make a call. I left mine in the other car."

"Who do you want to call at this hour?"

Boyd just looked at him. "You gonna give me the phone or not?"

Eric pulled out his phone. Boyd grabbed it, punched in a number and picked up still more speed as he waited for it to connect.

"Hey!" Eric protested. "Boyd! Slow the fuck down!"

"Chill," Boyd said, the phone still held to his ear. "Everything's under control."

Eric put on the seatbelt. Boyd was going seventy-five right through the downtown area, the streets of which were fortunately deserted. He wondered if Boyd was high. Then wished sharply that the possibility had occurred to him before he'd gotten into the car.

What a champ. He had succeeded in packing yet another display of shitty judgment into this night. Accepting a ride not from a stranger, but from an all too familiar asshole who had now proven to be stoned out of his fucking mind.

Yep, this one was a personal best.

"Yeah, it's me," Boyd said into the phone. "Uh huh…yeah. I'll be there soon… Yeah sure…okay…later."

Boyd didn't give Eric's phone back when he was done. He hung onto it and accelerated. Chilly air rushed through the open windows. They were heading downhill, picking up speed as they went toward the stoplight at the crossroads. It was red.

"Boyd!" he yelled. "Slow down!"

*Whoosh,* they sailed through the light at ninety-five. Boyd threw his head back and let out a long, guttural howl as the car thudded and bounced onto the metal roadway of the Kettle Canyon Narrows Bridge. Wind from the open windows roared in Eric's ears.

"Are you out of your fucking mind?" he yelled. "Stop this car! Let me out!"

"Don't be a pussy!" Boyd yelled back. "Don't you want

to see how this baby handles when you really open her up? You need to get on the highway for that!"

"No! I have shit to do! Let me out and give me my fucking phone back!"

Boyd let out a shrill laugh, and flung Eric's phone out the window. It sailed right over the railing of the bridge and down into the Kettle River.

Holy *fuck*. The guy was psychotic.

Eric leaned to look at the speedometer as they sped up onto the highway access ramp doing a hundred and five…no, one-ten…one-fifteen. Weaving madly from one side of the two-lane to the other. If he fought Boyd for the wheel, they would either hit the rock wall on one side and bounce off or else crash through the guard rail and fly off a cliff on the other.

He positioned himself to grab the wheel at the first opportunity…and then noticed that Boyd's hands were an unearthly, plasticky white. He was wearing latex gloves.

The *fuck?*

No time to wonder as the car sped on at those deadly speeds, shrieking around the tight turns. They passed the sign for Peyton State Park, ten miles out of town. There was a turn-off for a parking lot and a trailhead. Eric prepared to lunge for the wheel as soon as they approached the wider spot in the road—

Boyd slammed on the brakes just short of it, sending the Porsche into a wild spin. A full three-sixty and then some. They bounced off the jagged, rocky wall with a crunch.

Boyd bumped the battered car back up onto the roadway and jerked the car onto the exit to the trailhead parking lot at the last minute.

The Porsche shuddered to a stop next to a black pickup,

the only other vehicle in the lot. Boyd was panting, his lips drawn back from his teeth like a feral animal.

Pure hatred blazed out of his wild eyes as he stared at Eric.

"Boyd." Eric kept his voice low and calm. "Are you high?"

"Fuck you, man. Just…fuck you." Boyd shoved open the door and stumbled out. He lifted the tequila bottle high, and whipped it down against the open car door.

Glass shattered. Shards scattered over the car seat. Liquor soaked the steering wheel, the leather upholstery. Eric shoved open the door and leaped out of the car, poised to defend himself.

But Boyd didn't attack him. He just backed up toward the black pickup, eyes so wide open, the whites showed all around his blue irises. He stumbled into the door, groping for the handle. Opened the door and climbed in.

The motor revved, the lights went on. The pickup reversed with a violent lurch. It K-turned and thudded hard over the speedbumps as it sped out of the parking lot.

Eric stared after it, his mind blank. Shocked into stillness. The sound of the pickup's motor swelled as Boyd doubled back onto the highway, heading back toward Shaw's Crossing. The sound faded, giving way to utter silence.

Eric dragged his wits together after a moment. Forced himself to take stock of the situation.

It sucked. He was at Peyton State Park, with a badly damaged, tequila-soaked luxury Porsche that didn't belong to him. With no phone, and no clue. What the *fuck* had just happened?

He pulled the door open once again and opened the compartment under the dash and fished out the title and registration.

Benedict James Vaughan. Shock slowly gave way to horrified understanding.

Vaughan had set him up. He'd put Boyd up to this. Lured Eric into position by running off for the weekend and leaving Demi alone in the house, knowing that they wouldn't be able to resist such an opportunity for privacy.

What a fucking sleaze. If Vaughan thought that Eric was such dangerous trash, then he should be sticking close to home, protecting his precious girl with a shotgun. Not using her as bait. That was nasty. Lower than dirt.

It made him sick with rage, as much for Demi as himself.

Eric walked around the car, trying to stay calm. The cops might have already been set upon him. Chief Bristol had replaced Otis as police chief when Otis retired, but Otis wasn't going to intercede for him. He'd made that painfully clear.

Eric had to clean up his own damn messes.

He was going to face false accusations when he got back to town. One option was to walk back to town with the Porsche keys in his pocket. Go straight to the cops, tell them everything, and hope for mercy and understanding. But that would mean hours spent walking while his accuser had a head start. Reporting the car stolen. Establishing his story.

Option Two, he drove the Porsche to the nearest gas station, called the cops from the public phone and explained what happened. That option had the advantage of speed and immediacy. The faster he moved to defend his innocence, the better.

But he was being deliberately maneuvered into driving the damn thing, which was a trap in itself. Dinged up as it was, windows broken, soaked with liquor. He'd be truly fucked if he was seen or stopped driving it.

All his options looked shitty. But the more time he wasted dithering, the more poisoned against him the situation would be.

So, straight to the closest public phone. The Quik-Stop Gas-n-Go.

*Move, already.* Eric brushed the broken glass off the tequila-soaked leather seat and turned the key in the ignition. Accustomed as he was to the coughing, groaning, hiccupping Monster, the deep, mellow purr of the Porsche's powerful engine vibrated through his body, but he couldn't enjoy it.

He imagined Demi finding out. This whole thing had been organized to turn her against him. To make him look like a dangerous psycho.

That made him so murderously angry, he barely noticed the vehicle behind him on the highway. Not until he felt the *thump* and got nudged almost off the road.

He steadied the car, accelerating around a hair-pin curve to get away from it. A big Army green Humvee, riding his ass. *Bump. Bump.* The *fuck?*

That bastard was actually trying to run him off the road. Holy shit—*bump.*

He barely kept on the roadway this time. Now he was going as fast as Boyd had been driving just to stay ahead of his pursuer. The Humvee jammed into him on one side, sending him bouncing off the guard rail. Eric overcorrected, fishtailing on the dew-slicked asphalt—

*Crunch,* the Humvee got him a good one. He crashed against the guard rail again…

…and went through it. Right over the edge.

The world flipped, and green rushed past his eyes, branches snapping—

He stopped short with a hard jerk. Listened to rocks and dirt continuing to tumble and slide down the steep hillside, pattering down on the bottom of the car from above.

He was hanging upside down.

Empty space outside the window. Tree branches waved far, far below him. There was a stand of young trees clinging to the side of the hill that had stopped the Porsche in its slide. The driver's side of the car was pointed down—over a yawning nothing.

Water rushed, somewhere far below him. The seatbelt was all that held him in place. Men's voices. They were getting closer. One higher, more nasal, one low and growling.

"...to make sure he's dead." The high-voiced, nasal guy.

An indistinct snarling sound from the other one.

"I don't fucking care," the first guy said. "Hit him on the head with a rock, snap his neck, smother him, whatever the fuck you want. Just finish it."

More inaudible mumbling.

"Because I said so, asshole." The voice sounded impatient. "Climb down. Get it done."

It took a minute for it to sink in. When it did, Eric started struggling with the door. It had been warped in the crash, but by kicking and straining, he pounded it loose.

It swung heavily open, dangling straight down. The weight of it falling open caused a sudden shift in weight, making the car jolt and slide even further down the steep slope. It caught against still more slender new trees that looked too small to hold it. Some were already splintered and bent, about to give.

He blinked blood out of his eyes, and contemplated the empty space below. It was a long drop to the steep, rocky slope. When he hit it, he would bounce and then keep sliding right on down. Faster and faster. Nothing to keep him from rolling right off the cliff. From there, it was another long free-fall to the rocky bottom of the canyon.

That, or get killed by those guys who were crawling down here. He was in no condition to fight them. He was all fucked up.

He saw Demi in his mind's eye. At the waterfall. Drops of water sparkling in her thick black eyelashes. Her beautiful smile, shining in his mind like a faraway star.

He released the seatbelt and fell.

# 16

"He used you, sweetheart," Elaine Vaughan's voice caught in her throat. "I am so sorry. I wish that it weren't true, but it is."

"We warned you." Her father's face was a mottled red mask of fury. "We fucking warned you, but you had to blunder right into his trap."

Demi looked blankly from one parent to the other, and then to Chief Bristol, who had followed them into the kitchen. "Eric did…what?"

"You heard us the first time. He seduced you just to get inside this house. My goddamn house. You probably even gave him a tour. Elaine, did you check your jewelry box? I haven't even looked at the safe yet."

"Please, Ben, not now."

"That son of a bitch weaseled his way in, and when he'd had his fun with you, he took the keys off the board in the kitchen and made off with my Porsche. Those are the facts."

"I…I can't believe it," Demi said blankly. "It's just…it's

impossible."

"You have to believe it!" her father bellowed. "They found him in the wreckage! Or beneath it, anyway, in the streambed at the bottom of the canyon. Evidently he'd fallen out of the open car door when the car hit the trees."

She sucked in air, sharply. "Is he hurt?"

"Of course," Benedict snorted. "Of course, that's all you can think about."

Demi kept her eyes fixed on Chief Bristol until he answered.

"He's pretty banged up," the police chief admitted. "A concussion, cracked ribs, a broken wrist, various lacerations. He's lucky to be alive. Either the crash or the fall should have killed him, but it didn't. He'll recover."

"Worthless piece of shit can recover in jail," her father muttered.

"Where is he now?" she demanded. "Here in town?"

"No, they took him to Granger Valley for the trauma unit when they thought he might have internal bleeding. Turned out he didn't need it. No internal injuries."

"Just my luck," her father snarled.

"Ben, don't." Elaine's voice was sharp. "We don't need any more ugliness."

"She was the one who brought the ugliness in here, and took it to her bed. And then showed it where I kept my car keys."

"Is he conscious?" Demi cut in.

"No, no, no," her mother said hastily. "You're not going to see him. You can't."

"Mom, I just want to talk to—"

"You damn well won't. Hasn't he done enough? He's a degenerate. What was left of the car was soaked with tequila. I just hope you're not pregnant, or infected with some vile disease."

"Shut up, Dad," she said. "Your gross is showing."

"You still have the nerve to mouth off to me? After what you just did to me?"

Chief Bristol put down his coffee cup with a sigh and stood up. "Calm down, folks." He turned to Demi. "Don't try to see Eric. He's heavily sedated. And be honest with yourself. What could he possibly say to you right now that would be worth hearing?"

She opened her mouth to reply, and stopped. Unable to think of a single thing.

"Walk away," Chief Bristol urged her. "That's the best thing in these cases. Forget him and get on with it. You've got your whole life ahead of you."

"Yes, that's best," Elaine said. "I think Demi and I should leave town for a while."

"Demi has to make her statement," Chief Bristol said sternly.

"Of course, right away. Then we'll go to my sister Helen's summer place in New York, up on Long Island. Some time in a beach house sounds like just the thing. We'll be available by phone anytime you need to ask Demi anything. And your dad can join us later. After he's taken care of the, ah, details."

"What details?" Demi demanded, swiveling to stare at her father.

"Honey, it's just like the chief said. Walk away. It's a big mess, and nobody is going to talk about anything else for weeks in this town. You don't need to deal with that."

"I'm the one who was robbed," Dad said. "I'm the one pressing charges. You should just disappear. Please. Get gone.

I certainly don't want to look at you."

"Stop it, Ben," her mother hissed. "Once you've given your statement to the chief, we'll head to New York. Take in a few Broadway shows, do some shopping on Fifth Avenue, just the two of us, to take our mind off things. Then off to Aunt Helen's beach cottage in Bridgehampton. Won't that be relaxing?"

"But…my job at the—"

"I already talked to Raelene. She understands. In fact, she said it's probably for the best if you go. Don't worry about the job. That's the least of your worries."

Demi stared at her parents. Her father scowling. The anxious furrow between her mother's brows. Mom's lips were moving, but Demi couldn't hear the words.

Sounds had retreated behind a thick wall in her mind.

She'd been numb up to now, as if she were watching something on TV that didn't really touch her. Now the reality slammed into her with all its freezing, paralyzing force.

Dad was bellowing again, she had no idea about what, and couldn't bring herself to care. Chief Bristol was talking quickly, making *calm down* gestures with his hands.

*Just picture us together. It would be good.*

*He used you, sweetheart.*

*They found him in the wreckage.*

*You could blow me while I sit in the desk chair in the study.*

*What was left of the car was soaked with tequila.*

*I told you I love you, and I meant it.*

Phrases and fragments ricocheted around in her mind, but she kept seeing Eric's face when he held her in his car after their waterfall hike. The raw, shining look in his eyes when he told her that he loved her.

She pictured him in a hospital bed, bandaged up.

Bruised, battered and sedated. Maybe even handcuffed to a bedrail.

*I still want to run away with you.*

Oh, God, she wanted it, too. She wanted it so fucking bad. But he'd taken it away from her forever. Her shining fantasy, gone. He'd punished her by punishing himself.

It was spiteful and cruel and self-destructive, but if he'd wanted to hurt her to the core of her being, well, damn. Mission accomplished.

"…statement taken care of, then we throw some things into a bag and we're off." Her mother babbled on with forced cheerfulness. "I've already got our tickets. Our flight for New York leaves tomorrow morning. We'll stay in an airport hotel at SeaTac tonight."

She turned to her father, and the question just fell out of her mouth. "You just hate him so damn much," she said. "Even before all this happened. Why do you hate him so fucking much?"

"Watch your language!" her father snarled. "I think we've been more than vindicated in our low opinion of him!" His eyes darted toward Bristol, then back to her.

"Honey, we don't," her mother said anxiously. "We really don't hate him—"

"Bullshit." She pointed at her father. "He does. He went ballistic about Eric spending time with me even before all this mess. What aren't you telling me, Dad? I really want to know. Please. Clue me in."

"Honey," her mother said. "It may be tough to understand, but this is just a stupid thing that women do. All the time. They fall in love with a man's potential, not with who he really is. Even attractive, talented people with immense potential can be damaged beyond repair. It's almost like there are holes in their brain. You can't even blame them."

"But you can put them in jail, right?"

"Of course!" her father broke in. "He's a menace! He stole from me!"

"This thing you're saying about loving a man's potential, and holes in the brain," she said, looking at her mother. "That's not about Eric. You're talking about Dad."

"Demi!" Her mother's eyes widened. "Don't you dare!"

"You snotty bitch." Her father's chair screeched as he leaped up, face reddening.

"Like mother, like daughter," Demi went on. "We have the same weakness for screwed-up men, huh? The drinking, the tantrums, the secrets, the problems with Granddad. The mysterious phone calls he gets on those burner phones. The weird stuff with all that disappearing money at the Tacoma Distribution Center—"

"Stop it right there!" her mother said wildly. "Stop attacking us, Demi! We're just trying to protect you!"

"No you're not, Mom." Demi felt exhausted and empty. "You're protecting him." She pointed at Dad. "You always have. From Granddad, from himself, even from me. Because of the holes in his brain. He's like Swiss cheese, and he's always hated me for seeing it. I see right through him. Right, Dad? You just have to punish me for that."

"No! No, not at all! You're not making sense, honey." Her mother gave Chief Bristol a pleading look. "I'm so sorry you had to hear all this crazy nonsense, Chief. She's just so terribly upset."

"I didn't hear anything," the Chief said, putting down his coffee and rising to his feet. "I'll just be on my way, and leave you to continue your conversation in private."

They watched Chief Bristol hurry down the steps of the

side porch to his pickup, eager to get well away from the fucked up, toxic weirdness of the Vaughan home.

Mom rattled on anxiously, trying to cover the ominous silence with chatter. Demi heard the noise, but it took her a while before she could wrangle her brain into understanding the words. "…don't have much time, and you'll have to make the statement, too, so let's get the packing done and load up the car right away, okay?"

Demi stared at her mother for moment, and then she felt herself nod. Robotically.

She was going to feel like shit in any case. The where didn't matter. And a cottage on the beach in Bridgehampton was as far away as she could physically get from Eric Trask without crossing an ocean.

There was something to be said for that.

---

Eric kept struggling to rise to the surface, but any time he started to get close, another sting of the needle pulled him back down, screaming inside. Things were happening around him, things outside his control. Bad things.

At some point, he finally forced his eyes to open. For a moment, he saw Otis staring down at him, his face seamed and gray. Reddened eyes full of pain and worry.

Other times, he saw flashes of doctors, nurses. They did things to him. They hurt.

Finally his eyes opened and stayed open. He looked around, at the machines, the IV rack. Hospital bed. One of his arms had a cast. He followed the line that led from the IV bag down to the needle taped to his other arm. Tried to get that arm beneath him so he could sit up.

"Don't try that, son." A voice from behind him. "Stay

still. You need to heal."

He turned, and saw Chief Bristol lounging on a chair behind the IV rack.

"Hey, Chief," he said hoarsely. His tongue felt swollen and dry in his mouth.

"Finally awake," Chief Bristol said. "I've been coming in here to check on you for days, and damned if you didn't wake up right while I was here. That's handy."

"Guess so," Eric said. The attempt to speak sparked off a racking cough that hurt his ribs as if he were being beaten with a length of pipe.

When he finally managed to calm down the coughing fit, he whispered. "Otis?"

"Been and gone," Chief Bristol said. "Says he won't be back. He came to make sure you were actually alive, but he's pissed as hell at you. Says you're on your own."

Eric winced, and nodded. "I know."

"That Otis," Chief Bristol said. "Always the hard-ass. Mace and Anton were here nonstop while they were in town, but Mace got called out on a mission, and Anton had to go back to do some DJ tour or other. He'll be back. Hey there." Chief Bristol rose up and pushed him down into the bed as he struggled to rise. "Where do you think you're going?"

"I gotta get out of here," Eric said, his voice hollow. "I gotta talk to Demi."

"Wrong," Chief Bristol said. "You're staying right here. You are under arrest."

Eric stared at him, squinting. "Huh?"

"You have the right to remain silent," Chief Bristol began, and then proceeded to Mirandize him. Eric listened to the spiel, trying to breathe but it felt like the walls of the small hospital room were closing in around him. "What was I charged with?"

"Auto theft and driving under the influence. Jesus, Eric. I thought you were smart. You snowed me with those good grades and good SAT scores in high school." He shook his head, his mouth grim and tight. "Don't try to leave this room. You're weak as a kitten so I figured there's no need to cuff you. But if you make so much as a single move to leave this bed, I'll chain you to it until you're arraigned."

"I was set up," Eric said.

Chief Bristol shook his head sadly. "Here we go."

"I swear it," Eric said. "I was at Demi's house that night before it happened, yes, but I never took Ben Vaughan's car."

"You were fished out from underneath the wreckage," Bristol said. "Your blood is smeared all over the upholstery. Don't insult my intelligence."

"I am telling the truth," Eric said. "Do you want to hear my story or not?"

Bristol folded his beefy arms over his large belly. "Maybe you should talk to a lawyer before you start shooting off your mouth. You're still under the influence of sedatives. You have the right to a lawyer. It might be smarter to shut up and wait."

"My story isn't going to change," Eric said. "I remember everything. I can make a statement right now."

Chief Bristol recorded his account, and sat afterwards for several long minutes frowning at the wall.

"That's what you're going with?" he said. "Really? Boyd Nevins, who's never been in any trouble in his life, lures you into the car at four-thirty AM, throws your phone into the river, drives you to Peyton State Park and pours tequila all over you and Benedict Vaughan's Porsche. Evidently getting some of it into your mouth in the process, since the blood tests showed alcohol in your system—"

"I told you, Chief, I'd drunk some of it with Demi when I was at her house."

"And the less said about that, the better. Where were we? Oh yes, getting run off the road by mystery thugs who were trying to kill you. For no reason you can guess at."

"It sounds crazy," Eric said. "But it happened. Just like that. My fingerprints will be on the passenger side door, and Boyd Nevin's DNA will be on the neck of the tequila bottle at the trailhead at Peyton State Park, in the parking lot, right in front of the trailhead sign. If you look at the back end of the Porsche, maybe you can tell that another big car was ramming it. The paint on the Humvee was Army green. And there might be marks on the road where I went through the guard rail. Check it out. Please."

"I'll get the evidence techs on it," Chief Bristol said. "Henry Shaw is good friends with the judge who's likely to arraign you. The bail is going to be high. You'll go straight to the Granger Valley Correctional Facility for Men as soon as you're on your feet. Think long and hard about this, Eric. I'd be sorry to see you suffer more than you have already, but do not try to bullshit us. I know bullshit when I smell it. So will the judge."

Bristol was almost out the door when Eric sucked enough air into his sore chest to call out hoarsely. "Hey, Chief?"

Bristol turned slowly. "Yes?"

"Demi," Eric said. "Is she, uh…okay?"

Bristol's eyes hardened. Eric was almost sorry he'd asked.

"No, Eric," he said. "She did not look okay. She looked about how you'd expect a girl to look if some charming young asshole had seduced her and humiliated her and made big trouble for her with her family."

"I need to get a message to her," Eric said. "Could you tell her that I— "

"No. I wouldn't do it under any circumstances. And I couldn't in this case, because she's gone."

"Gone? Gone where?"

Chief Bristol snorted under his breath. "Like it's any of your business. Out of town. Far away from you. That's all you need to know. She doesn't want or need to talk to you ever again. Look to yourself. Leave Demi the hell alone."

He stepped through the door. The click of the door falling shut behind him jolted through Eric's cracked, aching bones like a gunshot.

# 17

*Three weeks later…*

Walking on the beach barefoot was the only activity Demi could stand these days. Every now and then she would jump in the water and fight the surging waves until they wore her out. Then she went back to walking. Far away from Mom's preaching and fussing. She was sunburned and wind-blown, staring out at the horizon with stinging eyes.

She tried not to think about it and failed miserably. He'd said he loved her. She'd felt the power moving them both when she heard the words. She'd felt so strongly that it was real. That he'd felt it, too. That magic couldn't be faked.

But in spite of those intense feelings, Eric hadn't been able to resist a random, vengeful impulse when he was angry. He really was that small and petty. That stupid.

It was a fucking tragedy. It made her physically sick. She could barely eat.

Mom kept saying that it was better to be disillusioned

now, right up front. Much better this way than after ten years and three kids. And Mom was right. About this, at least. If she could only stop thinking about Eric. Just for a few seconds at a time.

Hours of sun, waves crashing, wind roaring in her ears, day after day. It made her tired, and that helped. It got her through to her evening glass of wine or three, and Mom was too attached to her own evening glasses of wine to criticize Demi's. Small blessings.

She got back to where she'd left her towel and beach bag right before sunset, and looked around at the empty sand dune. It took a while to find her long abandoned beach towel, mystery novel and water bottle. They had been buried by blowing sand.

She unearthed them and shook out the sand. She retrieved the bike and made her way through the grid of roads through potato fields and luxury estates until she got to Aunt Helen's weathered gray cottage on the outskirts of Bridgehampton.

And saw another car parked next to Mom's rental. Dad was here. At last.

So. That meant plans had been finalized. Conclusions had been drawn. Tonight, she'd learn things about Eric's fate that she wasn't ready to know.

At the same time, she was pathetically desperate to know more.

Demi took a moment to steady her knees, trying to breathe calm into herself before she went inside. She found Dad and Mom sitting together at the kitchen table. He set down his glass of Scotch when he saw her.

"Hello, Demetra," he said stiffly. "You look very, ah…tan."

"Lots of beach time," she said inanely. "Hi, Dad."

She walked in, dropping the bag and pausing awkwardly in the kitchen.

"You're getting sand everywhere," her father said.

Mom popped up instantly. "I'll sweep it up."

"That's not the point, Elaine. The point is, as usual, she's not thinking. She's just barging along with no thought for anyone but herself."

"How's Eric?" Demi asked.

Her father looked irritated at being cut off in mid-rant. "How do you think? He's incarcerated. He's completely unrepentant. And he refuses to take the deal."

"What deal?" she asked.

"My lawyers offered him a very generous deal. If he pleads guilty, it's two years in a maximum security prison. Much better than the maximum of ten, to say nothing of the DUI. But he insists he's not guilty. It's stupid, considering his circumstances. If he had half a brain, he'd take the deal. But he doesn't, as we know, so it'll be ten years for him. The world will be a safer place once he's sentenced. For a while, at least."

Demi stared down at her sandy feet. She realized in that moment that she could not stay even one more night under the same roof as her father.

"Mom, I'm taking the last train back to the city tonight," she announced. "I'll stay at Aunt Helen's apartment. I'm flying to Seattle in a couple days, so I want to do a little last-minute shopping before I go."

"Yes, your mother said you'd booked a ticket," Dad said. "That's one of the reasons I hurried out here. To talk to you first."

"You didn't have to. We'd see each other on Thanksgiving. Or Christmas."

"Touching daughterly love," her father said sourly.

Demi gave him a stony look. "Really, Dad? You feel put upon? You want a remorseful daughter who's seen the error of her ways? Because I'm not feeling apologetic."

"Oh, God," her mother moaned. "You two are already at it, in less than five minutes. I can't take this. Ben, you promised you wouldn't!"

Dad ignored her. "You dodged a bullet, Demetra! You should be grateful! We tried to warn you, and you still have an attitude!"

"I was born with attitude, Dad."

"You're still angry at me for taking away your toy! That's all that a piece of meat like Eric Trask could ever have been to you!"

She retreated toward the stairs. "Excuse me," she said. "I need to pack."

"If you're so convinced that he deserves a second chance, you can give him one."

Demi froze in place, chilled by his tone. He sounded triumphant. Pleased with himself. When she turned to look, he wasn't smiling, but his eyes were bright with excitement. Mom's looked pained and fearful.

There was a trap here. A bad one.

"What's that supposed to mean?" she asked slowly.

"You can stop this whole process right now. If you choose to," her father said. "My lawyers will destroy him if he goes to trial. He'll get the maximum. Or…I could drop the charges. And he walks."

"Why would you do that?" Her suspicion was growing.

"To safeguard the future of my only daughter."

Dad's voice had taken on that hateful, sanctimonious

tone that drove her nuts.

"Stop with the riddles," she said. "Plain English, please."

"Okay," Dad said. "These are the conditions. Give up this stupid restaurant internship. Forget the Culinary Institute. Commit to a job at one of the Shaw Paper Products facilities. Swear to your grandfather that you'll prepare for leadership in his company. Swear that you will never contact that person again. Do all this, and he walks. Free to destroy his and other people's lives in some fresh new way, far from you."

Demi finally managed to close her mouth. "Wow," she said. "Just…wow."

"I think it's a very reasonable offer," Dad said.

Demi thought about it for a moment. "I thought you'd reached the maximum of manipulative bullshit, Dad. I was so wrong. You have surpassed yourself yet again."

"I would pass on the smart remarks, if I were you. You're in no position to make them."

"Is that part of your terms and conditions? I wash my mouth out with soap and be a smiling plastic doll from here on out?"

"No. I know that's too much to hope. I'll settle for not having you destroy your own future and prospects, which is embarrassing to watch. If this shit-show was useful for anything, it's this. Forcing you to behave like a reasonable adult, not a spoiled child."

"You hypocritical bastard," Demi said.

"Oh, God, honey," her mother moaned. "Please, stop. Is this hostility all I have to look forward to? For the rest of our lives?"

Dad's eyes were cold. "I'll be a bastard, if that's what it takes to manage her."

"I can't stand anymore of this." Her mother tossed back the rest of her wine, slammed the wine glass down and stomped out onto the patio.

Demi stared at her father. Marveling at him. Dad was prepared to use a man's freedom as leverage to jerk her around. Make her behave exactly as he wanted.

It was a devil's bargain. Working for Shaw's Paper Products would bore and suffocate her. It was light years from her dreams. The last thing she wanted.

But there was Eric, sitting in a cage for ten years.

She could just go her way. Be free and to hell with him. But she'd know, every day, every moment, that he was in there, trapped and miserable. She'd always be aware that she could have freed him. That constant awareness would poison her life.

It would be unbearable.

He deserved his fate. She hated that lying, thieving asshole for what he'd done. He didn't deserve this sacrifice from her.

But it didn't matter. She couldn't walk away and leave Eric Trask in prison.

"Okay, Dad." Her voice barely sounded like her own. "You win."

His eyes flashed, triumphant. "We have a deal?"

"Yes," she said.

"Call whoever is managing the internship," he said. "Right now. In front of me. Tell them you are declining it. After that, I'll call my lawyer and get things moving."

Icy clarity settled over her as she considered that. "You first," she said.

"Demi—"

"You've acted in bad faith before. You call the lawyer

first. Or else nothing."

Dad stared at her stonily. She held his gaze without blinking.

"Done," he said.

She picked up his smartphone and held it out. "It's still business hours on the west coast," she said. "Call now. And put it on speakerphone."

# 18

Eric blinked up at the blinding white sky as the prison gate ground slowly closed behind him. He stood there on the empty road after it closed with a hollow *clang*.

He still didn't believe it.

The news had come out of nowhere today. He'd been called in to talk to the warden.

*The charges have been dropped. You're free to go. Good luck.*

He put on the clothes they gave him. Anton or Mace must have left stuff at the hospital for him before they left. A sweatshirt, some jeans that hung too low on his hips since he'd lost weight. His work boots and socks. Nothing else.

The sweatshirt wasn't quite up to the frosty wind coming down off the mountains, but he wasn't complaining. He would have cheerfully walked out naked into a blizzard after two weeks in that place.

Vaughan had boxed him in. Every detail had been thought of to disprove his story. Boyd's alibi had been watertight. No traces of Army green paint had been found on the back of the Porsche. Even the smashed tequila bottle in the parking lot had disappeared before the evidence techs got there to examine it. All of it gone. Like it had never existed.

He'd been lying broken and sedated in a hospital bed while his enemies had all the time in the world to set the scene and tweak it just how they wanted it.

Now he was free. There had to be a catch. He kept looking over his shoulder, braced for who the fuck knew what.

A shot to the head, likely as not. Someone wanted him dead. And that was pretty severe even for a prick like Vaughan. Eric kept racking his brains to understand it, and kept coming up blank. Why kill him, for fuck's sake? He understood perfectly that he was not a promising prospect as a son-in-law, but hit men? Seriously? Goddamn.

Still. Death out in the open air was preferable to prison. After all, death could find him in there, too. Even more easily. In prison, there was nowhere to run.

There was no one at the gate to meet him. There had been no warning. Mace was off on a Force Recon mission. Anton was in Vegas working. Otis was being a hard-ass.

Anton had come to see him in jail. At the end of his visit, he'd leaned over the table and murmured, "You know that if this goes south, Mace and I will bust you out."

"Don't say it," Eric said, through clenched teeth. "Do not fuck your lives up just because I fucked up mine."

"I like a challenge." Anton's eyes had that eager glow that made him uneasy. "Say the word. We'll come down on this place like a sledgehammer. It'll be beautiful."

Eric allowed him to imagine it for a few amazing seconds…and then shook his head. "Let's work the system first."

"The system fucked you, brother. You want to play that

game, fine. You can play it. But keep in mind that it's just a game. Whenever you're ready, your own personal army of the faithful will come in here and fuck them up so hard. Anytime, man. Anytime."

Eric hadn't seen Anton's eyes look so lit-up in years. Not since the night they spirited Fiona away from Kimball. This latest clusterfuck had stripped away the thin veneer of civilization his brother had put on since GodsAcre.

Twenty long miles of winding highway from Granger Valley to Shaw's Crossing. No cash for a bus. Hitchhiking never worked for him. He was too physically intimidating.

From the highway exit, he cut cross country and hiked over the ridge to Otis's place, turning eleven miles to six. Even so, his legs shook and ached from exhaustion and his injuries from the accident. It was after sunset when he stumbled up to Otis's house.

It was deserted. Otis's truck was gone. The house was dark. As he got closer, he saw the Monster parked out behind the shed. Her tires were entirely gone now, and her windshield had been smashed into tattered, milky cobwebs of caved-in glass.

There was a small pile of stuff at the top of the porch steps. A rolled up Army blanket, a tarp and a backpack. In it was a flask of water, MRE military rations, matches, soap, a spoon, a pocketknife and a small, battered saucepan. A duffel bag had all of his clothing shoved into it. His laptop, tablet, cables and drives were on top of them. An envelope with his documents. Passport, military ID, driver's license. Even his library card.

On top of the whole thing, weighed down by a rock, was an envelope. Inside were seven twenties, a five, and some change, and a sheet of paper with just a few words scrawled on it, in Otis's jagged handwriting.

*Cashed your paycheck. Don't bother the girl. She doesn't want to hear from you.*

*OT*

He tried the front door. Locked. He checked the place in the loose board behind the bird feeder under the maple where Otis had always left a spare key. No key to be found.

He was not welcome in the house. Otis didn't want to see his face. He hadn't seen Otis since that brief, drug-addled glimpse of him in the hospital. The MREs, water, blanket and money was as close to a love note as he was ever going to get.

He'd take it and be grateful.

He camped in the deep woods that night just over Otis's property line, out of respect for his adopted father's banishment. He made a fire, ate an MRE, drank up all the water, then slept like a dead man wrapped in the blanket.

In the morning, he loaded up the duffel and pack for the long slog back into town. He stopped when he got to Kettle River and used the soap Otis had given him to wash up. Tried not to think of Demi's eyes when he looked at the blue-green water. Demi's ring.

When he had to leave the cross-country route and get onto the roads, cars slowed down as they passed him. People gawking, rubbernecking. He was a local spectacle.

He didn't make eye contact as he walked to the bus station. No one spoke to him.

A bus was leaving for Tacoma. From there, he'd get one to Las Vegas.

In spite of Otis's warning, he tried to contact Demi with his laptop with the first free Wi-Fi he found. He'd written her letters every day from prison. No reply.

Online, he found himself blocked from all her social

media accounts. He'd tried calling the phone number she'd given him, but it was no longer in service.

It could drive a man to desperation. But a few weeks in jail had taught him a lot about desperation. The dust-and-ashes taste of that place was fresh in his mouth.

He wouldn't risk going back. He couldn't force her to listen to him.

He spent the bus journey in a nightmare-studded doze. Watching the country speed by when his eyes were open, drifting into uneasy dreams when they weren't. Sometimes he saw Demi's face. Sometimes it was the Hummer, nudging the back of his car over a cliff.

Sometimes he defaulted to his classic stress flashback standby. The flames, people screaming. Trees ablaze, like huge torches in the dark.

He got to Las Vegas at four-thirty in the morning, blowing his last few bucks on a taxi to Anton's place. He buzzed his brother's intercom, staring up into the camera.

A burst of static, then, "Holy shit. You're already here? Come on up."

The gate snapped open, and Eric made his way up the stairs. Anton's apartment was one side of a big building with a central courtyard that featured a garden of desert plants. The cacti looked eerie and alien down there in the dim, moody lighting.

Anton's front door was ajar. Eric pushed his way in, and stopped when he saw a leggy redheaded woman perched on a chair, struggling with the strap of her sandal.

She was stunning, but in his current wrecked state, her sequined, stiletto-heeled glory was an assault on his burning eyes.

She blinked at him rapidly with big dark eyes and

tossed her fiery mane of curls back with practiced grace. "Whoa," she said throatily. "Crystal, check this one out. Who the hell are you, big boy?"

An equally impressive blonde, this one in a stretchy black-beaded sheath, sashayed out of the kitchen and looked him over with cool, professional interest. "Hello, there."

Eric looked from one to the other. "Uh…this is Anton Trask's apartment, right?"

The girls looked at each other and laughed. "It most definitely is, honey," Crystal said. "So you're the reason he's tossing us out? What, are you his brother? You're so big and tall and thick, like him. Just skinnier."

"Hot like him, too," the red-head observed, raking him from head to toe. "Nice."

Anton appeared at the top of a spiral staircase, wearing only half-buttoned jeans. It left the extensive tattoo art all over his thickly muscled torso on full display.

His eyes flicked from Eric to the girls who were still blatantly ogling him. "Still here, ladies?" Anton said. "I told you that the car was waiting."

"You can't rush me," the red-head said, pouting. "It takes a while to work a dress this tight back onto my body."

"Your dress looks fine, Mandi," Anton told her. "Goodnight."

Mandi rolled her eyes. "Don't be a dick. So who's the new guy? What's his deal?"

"He's tired from a long trip." Anton's voice was cool and remote. "He doesn't want to play. Out you go. Tomorrow is another day."

Mandi sighed sharply. "Fine, we'll fuck off, then. Later, babe. Come on, Crystal."

They filed out the door, giving him the eye as they left.

Their high-pitched giggling echoed down the corridor outside after the door shut behind them.

Eric stared at his brother. "That's the kind of woman you bring home?"

Anton's eyes narrowed. "Don't judge my choice of sex partners, you fucking prude. Keep in mind, I haven't gotten myself thrown off any cliffs or tossed into any prisons lately because I rolled around in bed with Crystal and Mandi."

Eric let the pack and duffle bag fall to the floor with a rattling thud as exhaustion settled over him. "You have a point," he conceded.

"Damn right," Anton said. "Actually, I don't usually bring women here at all. But I was too buzzed after my set to make it all the way down to the hotel suite. I got lazy."

"Hotel suite? What hotel suite?"

"For sex," Anton explained. "I keep one rented downtown. So I don't have to drag the girls out of bed and throw them out, like I did just now. In the hotel suite, I can just get up and leave myself. Way easier and less embarrassing for everyone concerned."

"Sounds cold," Eric said.

"It is. But like I said, you're in no position to offer relationship advice."

The look on Eric's face made his brother frown. He gestured at the bar. "You look like shit. Want a drink? Scotch, vodka, bourbon, tequila—"

"No tequila," Eric blurted.

Anton nodded. "I'll get you a beer," he said. "Come on into the kitchen."

Eric slumped on the table. Anton placed a cold beer in front of him and pulled a platter out of the fridge heaped with finger food that looked like it had come off a catering tray. He got right to work grilling him an enormous ham and cheese sandwich.

"Eat," Anton urged. "You must have lost what, thirty pounds? You look like hell for a man who just got his life back against all odds. Is it because of the girl?"

Eric stared down at his beer. "She changed her cell number," he said bleakly. "Blocked me on the socials. I sent her letters through the mail from prison. No reply."

"Of course not," Anton said.

"I just want to explain," Eric said. "I want her to hear my side. That's all."

"Suck it up." His brother's voice was uncompromising. "You're not going to get that satisfaction. Chalk a point up for the bad guys. Be glad you're still in the game at all."

Eric shook his head. Every part of him screamed in protest, but arguing was stupid when you knew you were wrong.

"I've got your room ready," Anton said. "Back bedroom, end of the hall upstairs. I had the housekeeper make up the bed for you. You've got four job interviews tomorrow. The earliest is at six PM, so you can rest up first. Security jobs at the casinos and clubs. To tide you over until you're back on your feet. With your military record and my recommendation, they're all going to want you, so go where the showgirls are hottest."

"How did you know I was on my way here to you?"

"Otis told me," Anton said.

"Otis wasn't there when I got home," Eric said. "He left my stuff outside."

"He's too ticked off to talk to you, but he's been climbing the walls ever since your accident. He thought that you were done for when they tossed you in the joint."

"He didn't believe me," Eric said bleakly. "About Boyd. And the Hummer."

"Nope. Otis couldn't wrap his head around that. It was too crazy for him."

Eric braced himself. "What about you and Mace? Was it too crazy for you guys?"

Anton flipped the grilled sandwich. Melted cheese sizzled loudly on the surface of the pan. "Dude, please," he said evenly. "We're from GodsAcre. Crazy is mother's milk for us. Besides, we saw the condition you were in. You were out of your head for that girl. You would never have risked that just for a fucking joyride. Plus, you've never told a lie in your life, except the night we were smuggling Fiona out of GodsAcre, and even then you sucked at it. So yeah, we believe you. Mace and I are Team Eric. Do or die."

Eric's covered his eyes with his hand. They stung. Those words made him feel like he could almost start to breathe again. "How did Otis know I was coming here?"

"Irma Stubbs at the bus station called him right after you bought your ticket. Otis called me up and gave me all kinds of instructions about how to manage you, what to say to you. I won't inflict them on you right now."

"I appreciate that," Eric said.

"He called again to tell me he'd wired some money for you," Anton went on. "Then he called a third time to put the fear of God into me about not telling you that the money was from him. There's a thousand bucks on the dresser in that back bedroom. Do not ever tell him I told you that he sent it. I don't want him mad at me, too."

"I'll never get the chance to tell him now," he said bleakly.

"Bullshit," Anton said. "He'll mellow out. He still

thinks it's his job to provide boundaries. Like when we were in high school. Was that ever a goat-fuck."

"It was," Eric agreed.

"But we got through it," Anton said, sliding the golden, fragrant sandwich out onto a plate and slicing it in half. "Otis kept us from blowing up buildings or slitting throats or ripping out guts. He did it by being a hard-ass, and now he can't stop being one."

"I know."

Anton placed the sandwich in front of his brother. "And also, by the way. For what it's worth, Otis hates that butt-wipe Ben Vaughan with a white-hot fiery passion."

Anton sat down opposite him and silence fell as his brother watched him eat. He didn't say another word until Eric had eaten every bite.

Then Anton took a long pull on his beer, and finally spoke. "Let's kill him."

His brother's tone was so casual, Eric could hardly believe he'd heard right. For an instant, he let himself entertain the idea. It acted like gasoline on the embers of his rage.

He tamped it down. "No," he said grimly. "That's not who we are."

"That lying shithead slandered you and got you fired," Anton said. "He framed you for car theft. Put a contract out on your life. Had you wrongfully imprisoned. Fuck that guy. He doesn't deserve to keep on breathing."

"Please," Eric said. "Don't tempt me."

"The world would be better off without him. Mace is on board. Let's do it."

Eric shook his head.

Anton looked frustrated. "Remember at GodsAcre,

after we got Fiona out? You and Mace decided to kill that motherfucker Kimball after he flogged me. You would have followed through if the fire hadn't done your work for you. How's this any different?"

"I didn't know what prison was like then, for one thing," Eric said. "Plus, we wouldn't have been destroying anyone's lives by wiping out Kimball. Vaughan has a wife, a family. I couldn't do that to Demi. I've done enough damage to her life already."

Anton grunted. "What an altruist. All this regard for Vaughan's wife, who hates you, and Vaughan's daughter, who dropped you and dodged you and blocked you."

"I don't blame her," Eric said. "Any sane, reasonable person who isn't you or Mace would have concluded that I'm a dangerous dickhead moron with no impulse control. That was the whole point of this drama. She's scared of me now."

"I just want to take out the trash," Anton said. "We'd be doing the world a favor."

"Me, too. But that's old Jeremiah yammering in our heads. This isn't Jeremiah's world. We aren't establishing dominance in a blasted apocalyptic hell-scape. We're trying to integrate into society, remember? We follow their rules, we keep our noses clean, and we win anyway, because we have the stuff. Remember all Otis's lectures?"

Anton just barely cracked a smile. "Yeah. Getting preached at seems to be our fate. First Jeremiah, then Otis."

"We made a pact," Eric said. "Let's hold to it. We're going to crush it. All three of us. No excuses, Prophet's Curse and all. But we won't get very far if we start killing the people who piss us off. That violates the pact."

Anton took a swig of his beer. He still looked rebellious. "I started fantasizing about killing that prick after I visited you in jail," he admitted. "I was so angry."

"Yeah, me, too. But killing Vaughan isn't worth prison time. Trust me on this. I don't want you or Mace to learn that firsthand. And then there's Otis. Remember all the assholes who tried to persuade him we were psychopaths and that taking us in was too dangerous? We'd prove them all right. We can't do that to Otis."

Anton frowned. "We'd be smart about it. He'd never know."

"Like hell. Anything happened to Vaughan, Otis would be all over our asses."

Anton acknowledged that truth with a frustrated sigh. "Fine," he growled. "Vaughan gets a pass. Lucky bastard. For Otis's sake. But I still fucking hate it."

Eric leaned on the table, covering his eyes with his hand again. He couldn't stand eye contact with his brother. Not without shaking into pieces.

The weight of Anton's hand rested on his shoulder. "Hey," he said. "Dude. Fuck the Curse."

Eric nodded. "Yeah," he said wearily. "I know. Fuck the Curse."

"It won't get you. Not today. And not ever. We will crush this, bro," Anton said. "Because we know the secret."

Eric rubbed his eyes. "Secret? Right now I don't know jack-shit."

"You know this." His brother's fingers dug into his shoulder. "Jeremiah's prime rule, remember? Don't flinch from pain. It makes you fucking invincible."

Eric looked up at his brother. Their shared past flashed between them, buzzing in the air like a bolt of electricity. Shocking old memories to life. They hurt.

He forced himself to feel what lay beneath the years

that had passed since GodsAcre. Feeling it all, like Anton said. It was hard not to flinch away from it.

The GodsAcre fire was always burning in there. The screams of the dying echoed endlessly in his ears. The smell of smoke and charred flesh, always present in his mind.

He'd tried to hide it from Demi, but it wouldn't have stayed hidden forever. Ben Vaughan had only speeded up the inevitable.

The Prophet's Curse cast a long shadow. He would never get out from under it.

There was nothing left to do but show all those assholes just how badly they had underestimated him. Car theft, his ass. As if he needed to steal other people's shit.

They had no idea what he was capable of. But the world was going to find out.

*Maybe Demi would find out, too.*

No. Fucking…*no.* He couldn't let his mind go there.

Eric looked Anton straight in the eyes and raised his bottle. "To not flinching."

"Invincible," Anton repeated, lifting his beer.

They clanked bottles and drank deep.

# EPILOGUE

*Seven years later…*

Eric Trask looked out the floor-to-ceiling wall of glass of his private office at the sweeping view of the Golden Gate Bridge, wreathed in morning fog. He'd chosen this site for the San Francisco headquarters of Erebus, Inc. specifically for that view.

It relaxed him, which was rare. When he found something that worked for him, he took it.

The phone buzzed in his drawer. During his early morning deep focus sessions, he programmed it to ring only if Mace, Anton, or Otis called. But this wasn't their usual call time.

He opened the drawer with the fingerprint lock and answered. "Hey. Anton."

"Chief Bristol's been trying to reach you." His older brother's tone was harsh. "Your people won't put him through. Neither will your fucking cell phone."

Cold dread stabbed through him. "My people and my

phone are both trained not to bug me when I'm working. What's up?"

"Fuck," Anton muttered. "So I get to be the lucky bastard who tells you this."

Eric lowered himself down into his chair. His legs felt hollow. "Say it."

"Bristol called me," Anton said. "Otis had a stroke. At his house, sometime last night. They took him to the ICU."

"How is he?"

Anton didn't speak for moment. "He's gone." His brother's low voice was thick, almost unrecognizable. "He's dead."

Anton kept talking, but sound had retreated to someplace far away. Eric couldn't hear it over the ringing in his ears. The roaring, crackling sound. He closed his eyes and saw trees burning like torches.

"…his voice message, but I didn't get it in time." Anton's voice was audible again.

"Message? What message?"

"Check your voicemails. Otis left one for me and Mace around two o'clock last night. He must have left one for you. Go listen to it."

Eric opened up his voicemail. There was a message for him from Otis, dated two-eleven AM.

*Hey. Otis here. You boys need to come home. Soon as possible. All of you. Got things to tell you about GodsAcre. Can't say it on the phone. I'll explain when you get here. Bye now."*

The sound of Otis's gruff voice made his throat seize up.

Eric clicked back to the call. "I heard it, but I don't know what it means."

"Me neither. I heard it after I finished my set at the club

at four in the morning. I've been trying to call him ever since. Until Bristol reached me. He told me that Otis was dead by the time they got him to the hospital."

The sound of his brother's voice retreated once again. Eric pressed the smartphone to his ear, trying to hear his brother's voice over the crackling sound. His hands were cold, but his face was burning hot. Billows of heat felt like they were pressing against it. A cloud of flying sparks seemed to drift in front of his face.

"...Otis's house by this evening, but Mace won't be able to get there until tomorrow at the latest. Probably late tomorrow. He's trying to get a flight from Nairobi now. When can you get there?"

He struggled to focus. "If I start now, I could be there by late tonight."

Anton paused. "You'll come for real, right? You won't bail on me? I know you hate that fucking place like hell itself."

Eric's jaw tightened. He hadn't been in Shaw's Crossing since his troubles with Demi Vaughan and her family. And his brief but memorable stint in prison.

But Demi wouldn't be there. She'd be seven years gone. And he could face all the rest of those lying, thieving, murdering motherfuckers. Face them and smile.

"I'll be there," he heard himself say, before closing the call.

A knock sounded on the door. "Come in," he said.

Milo, one of his personal assistants came in, crisp and fresh, his white shirt adorned with a red bow tie. "Good morning, Mr. Trask." He put a tray on the worktable that held a gleaming chrome carafe and a cup. "Your coffee. Shall I put in an order to the kitchen for your breakfast?"

"No, thank you."

"Okay, then." Milo whipped out his tablet and stylus. "For messages, you have…let's see…three calls from a Chief Wade Bristol requesting an urgent call back, and then from last night, there are calls from Christina Spano, Astrid Kohl, Laurel Schissinger and Margot Paget. Do you need any of their numbers?"

Eric shook his head. All women he'd slept with in the past few weeks. Not today.

"As for your appointments this morning…let's see, first up, you have a meeting with Senator Ames at ten-thirty to discuss industry regulations for—"

"Cancel it," he said.

Milo looked shocked. "Cancel the Senator?"

"Death in the family. I have to leave town. Please let everyone know."

Milo gasped. "Oh, Mr. Trask, that's terrible. I'm so very sorry for your—"

"Thanks, Milo. Pack a case with all the equipment I might need to set up a remote workstation, and do it fast. I need to go home, grab some clothes and get on the road."

"Ah, yes, of course," Milo said hastily. "I'll get right on it."

"I'll get one of the cars from the garage and meet you out in front."

Eric walked through the quiet Erebus, Inc. building. Most of his employees had not yet started their day, but the place would fill up soon and be a buzzing hive of activity.

Once in the garage, he stood for a moment, undecided between his Mercedes SUV and his black Porsche GT3.

He chose the Porsche, and pulled out into the landscaped roundabout in front of the main entrance just as Milo emerged, hauling two big black plastic hard cases full of gear.

He popped open the front trunk. Milo hoisted the cases into it and then approached Eric's car window as he buzzed it down. "Drive carefully, Mr. Trask."

"Will do. Hey, Milo?"

"Yes, sir?"

"Do you smell smoke?"

Milo squinted as he sniffed the air. "No, just pine trees. It rained last night."

"Okay," he muttered, as the window hummed closed. "Later."

Driving a black Porsche GT3 991 into Shaw's Crossing after what had happened there seven years ago was not smart, he reflected as he pulled away. He'd be giving them all the finger. It was blatantly provocative. Arguably insane.

But fuck it. A man did what he had to do.

Otis would not have approved. But Otis wouldn't be there to see it.

He had to fight fire with fire.

**Want more? Demi and Eric's tale hurtles onward in Headlong, The Hellbound Brotherhood Book Two, which takes up their story seven years later...**

**ON SALE FEBRUARY 21, 2020!**

**Turn the page to read the first chapter!**

# HEADLONG
# THE HELLBOUND BROTHERHOOD

***They were never supposed to leave alive… Find out why New York Times bestseller Maya Banks hails McKenna's books as "A non-stop thrill ride..."***

**Only one woman could tempt him to return…**

**Eric Trask** and his brothers turned their backs on their past and forged successful futures for themselves. Only their beloved foster father's funeral could drag them back to the small town of Shaw's Crossing and its bad memories of GodsAcre, the doomsday cult deep in the mountains where they were raised, and the deadly fire that destroyed it. Only one memory still shone bright in Eric's mind—Demi Vaughan, with her lush, sexy mouth and her stunning green eyes. Their hot fling seven years ago had crashed and burned in the worst possible way. She's still mortally pissed at him…and more gorgeous than ever.

**Second chances…**

**Demi Vaughan** had done her best to forget Eric Trask. They told her from the start that he was a train wreck, and she hadn't listened. He'd broken her heart and derailed her life, and she'd be damned if she'd let him do it again, not now that she'd finally followed her dream and opened her own restaurant. But the years have only turned Eric into a more concentrated version of what he'd always been—a flint-eyed, ambitious, focused alpha male hunk. Just taller. Harder. And as intoxicating as hell.

Demi tries to withstand Eric's magnetic pull, but she can't resist the all-consuming heat between them. But an old evil still lies low in Shaw's Crossing, and Eric's arrival has shocked it back into life.

**Now it's not just their hearts that are in danger. It's their lives…**

**Visit me at my website, http://shannonmckenna.com for news and updates, but the best way to stay in touch is to subscribe to my newsletter! Here's the link, http://shannonmckenna.com/connect.php, so you'll never miss a new book or a great promo! Plus, look out for a special gift from me to subscribers…a free Obsidian Files novel!**

**Turn the page for a taste of Headlong…**

# HEADLONG

## 1

Eric Trask stared over Otis's flower-heaped coffin. His jaw ached from clenching his teeth.

He couldn't skip his adoptive father's funeral, but couldn't help reflecting that this display was a huge waste of extreme discomfort. The old man was gone. He couldn't appreciate the gesture, and no one else around here gave a flying fuck if Eric was present or not, other than his brothers Mace and Anton, who stood on either side of him.

They hated funerals like he did. For all the same reasons.

Yet here they were. Shoulder to shoulder, grim and stoic as befitted the sons of the Prophet, as well as sons of Otis Trask. Both those men had been heavy into grim stoicism.

A big crowd of Shaw's Crossing inhabitants had trooped down to the cemetery in the frigid wind for Otis's interment, which wasn't that surprising. Otis had been the chief of police in Shaw's Crossing for many years and had been highly respected in that role.

Some of those people were giving the Trask boys the

side-eye from across Otis's open grave. Not that they gave a shit.

No side-eye coming from Demi Vaughan, though. She didn't look at him at all.

Eric hadn't expected to see Demi here in Shaw's Crossing. He would have thought she'd be long gone, as far from her asshole of a father as it was possible to get.

But here she was, right in front of him. No time to prepare. To brace himself.

Looking at Demi gave him a hard, twisting ache in his chest. Different and distinct from the pain and shock of losing Otis. The feeling surprised him. He'd thought all that stuff from the past was buried deep and covered with concrete. He'd gone to great lengths to bury it. He'd even congratulated himself on how completely he'd gotten over it.

He hadn't. Like he needed anything else to humble him today.

On the plus side, being ignored by Demi left him free to discreetly ogle her, which was well worth doing. Seven years hadn't dimmed her glow. She hadn't gotten any taller, but her small frame had filled out, and every part of it looked great. Her full lips were painted a hot red and her long brown ringlets fluttered in the gusts of wind. He keenly remembered her hair's satiny softness and scent.

She looked sexy and tough in her snug black skirt. Black tights on her strong, shapely legs. High-heeled boots. A nipped-in black leather bomber jacket. Hot.

She still had that regal, indomitable look he remembered so well in those striking, pale green eyes. Clear, challenging. Demi Vaughan stared the world down fearlessly, calling out any bullshit she saw for what it was. Including Eric's own.

It had made him hard, when it wasn't driving him

fucking nuts. Sometimes both at the same time.

Demi stared at Otis's casket, not sparing him a glance, but Benedict Vaughan, her asshole father, made up for it with an unwavering glare.

Eric gazed right back. A look that silently said ever*ything he needed it to say.*

*I know what you did. I know what you are, you lying* piece of shit. And so do you.

Ben Vaughan's mouth twisted. His eyes slid away.

Vaughan himself, unlike Demi, didn't look so good. Seven years ago he could still have been called a good-looking guy, but not anymore. His face was puffy and bloated. His eyes bagged, his jowls sagged. Demi's granddad Henry Shaw, acknowledged king and boss of Shaw's Crossing, stood with them, but old man Shaw didn't glower at Eric. He just gazed at Otis's coffin with hollow, reddened eyes, hunched and sad in his black wool coat. Henry Shaw and Otis had served in Vietnam together. Marines. They went way back.

Eric forced himself to look away. Eye contact with the Vaughan/Shaw family was unwise. His long-ago fling with Demi had ended about as badly as a fling could.

Which was to say, with him in jail, looking at eight to ten. It had been a near thing.

Mace tapped his arm. "Pinstripes and hair grease at three o'clock," he said under his breath. "What's wrong with this picture?"

Eric spotted the guy instantly when he looked in that direction. He should have noticed the man already, but he'd been shamefully inattentive. Wandering down memory lane, gawking at Demi's hypnotic green eyes. He tried without success to place the stranger. A new arrival, a visiting relative, somebody's new out-of-town boyfriend?

No. 'Professional asshole' came off the man like a bad smell. He had shifty snake eyes. A hook nose. Balding, with a greasy black widow's peak. Bad skin, a pimp suit, and a restless, seedy urban vibe that was all wrong for Shaw's Crossing.

"His buddy's at nine o'clock," Anton whispered.

Eric assessed the other guy. Bigger than the first, beefy and bearded and thick in the neck. Cold, shuttered eyes. A brainless thug in a suit. The two were a matched pair.

"Assholes that Otis sent to jail?" he speculated under his breath.

"Maybe," Mace said. "Come to gloat over his corpse."

"If it was just one, maybe," Anton replied, his voice barely audible. "Not two. Bet they're packing."

"Yah think?" Mace said. "Good. Let's separate these shitheads off from the herd after and pick a fight with 'em. I need to vent."

The hungry flash of eagerness in his younger brother's eyes made Eric nervous. "No," he hissed. "We talked about this. In and out. No drama. Stick to the plan."

He forced his attention back to the service. The familiar verses made his stomach clench, just like the drone of the organ and the sickly smell of lilies at the funeral home. Otis's sister-in-law Maureen had organized all of that.

But when they lowered the coffin into the ground…God, he dreaded that part.

Eric and his brothers had declined to give a eulogy, their memories of Otis being their own damn business, so the eulogy had been given by the man who replaced Otis as chief of police after his retirement, Wade Bristol. Big, beefy guy in his late fifties. Eric remembered him all too well. Bristol had been the guy who arrested him and read him his rights while

Eric was lying in bed in the Granger Valley Hospital Intensive Care Unit.

He didn't hold it against the guy. Bristol had just been doing his job to the best of his ability.

The eulogy Bristol gave wasn't bad. Comprehensive. No surprises. Bristol droned on about Otis's courage, his exemplary life, his heroic and highly decorated military service, his selfless dedication to the community of Shaw's Crossing, etc., etc. All of which was absolutely true and could not be overstated, even if you tried.

Only Eric, Anton and Mace heard the subtext. Thirteen years ago, everyone had told Otis he was a goddamn lunatic for taking on a three-headed monster like Eric, Anton and Mace, after all the bad shit that gone down at GodsAcre. Just because it was the right thing to do, and nobody else seemed to be willing to do it.

Taking not one, not two, but three big, strong, massively fucked-up teenage boys with extensive combat training and a bizarre upbringing into his home…it was a disaster waiting to happen. Otis would be murdered in his bed. Everyone was sure of it.

But they hadn't hurt Otis. The old man was tougher than boot leather. He'd kept them in line. They'd all survived. It hadn't been easy, but Eric and his brothers had kept it together. Graduated from high school. Eric and Mace had even gone on into the military.

It was afterwards that everything had gone to shit. When Eric ran afoul of Benedict Vaughan and Henry Shaw for daring to raise his eyes to their precious princess.

And not just his eyes. Another part had risen up, as well.

Bad scene, all around. But in spite of everything, sex dreams about Demi Vaughan regularly jolted him out of sleep, panting and sweating and stone hard.

He'd gotten well away from that fucking place after the charges were dropped. Started his life fresh, far away from Shaw's Crossing. He'd worked like a bastard. So had his brothers, each in his own way. They'd promised not just Otis, but also each other. They would not be defeated.

They would make something out of themselves. Prove all the shitheads wrong.

They'd done it, for the most part. Built good careers. Lives for themselves, such as they were. Strange but true. They owed it all to Otis. Boot-leather tough, cantankerous, lecturing Otis.

It still seemed impossible that he could be gone. A stroke, they said, but Otis had gotten himself checked out, and recently. He'd bragged to them about being as healthy as a horse for his age. Just some arthritis. No reason that he wouldn't go on being his own ornery, opinionated, difficult self for decades to come.

And suddenly he was gone. With no warning except for that strange voicemail he'd sent to the three of them the night before his death. Not one of them had managed to get back to him in time.

He hadn't said that he was sick. Just that he had something urgent to tell them about GodsAcre, and that they needed to be in Shaw's Crossing to hear it. He'd sounded agitated. Afraid, even. Insofar as it was impossible to imagine Otis afraid.

But the mystery message had never been delive*red. Otis had died on his own dining room* floor. No warning.

Like all the people in the death cluster.

He tried not to dwell on that, but the thought hung heavy in the air and Eric was sure he wasn't the only person thinking it. Thirteen years ago, right before the GodsAcre fire, fourteen people in Shaw's Crossing had dropped dead in the course of only twelve days. All deaths had been unexpected, but there was no evidence of foul play. Like Otis.

Perfectly natural deaths…but for their suspicious timing.

The Prophet's Curse, the town called it. Sometimes to their faces.

It was the creaking of the ropes as they lowered Otis's casket down that set him off. Eric started struggling to breathe. His chest was being crushed in a vise. His head roared, his heart thudded, his belly heaved.

He heard coffin ropes in his nightmares. Thirteen years ago, they'd laid the victims of the GodsAcre fire to rest. So many coffins. All of them closed. By necessity, since the thirty-eight bodies inside them had been charred beyond recognition.

Nine of those coffins had been very *small.*

He felt like a container swiftly filling up with icy liquid. Fuck. After all these years, and it still got to him, as bad as it ever was. His throat w*as closing, che*st squeezing, no air, vision dimming. Heart thudding, boom boom boom.

Guilt, clawing inside him. For surviving it. Not being able to save them.

"…Trask? Mr. Trask? Excuse me? Sir?"

The funeral director spoke with the tone of someone who'd asked the question more than once. When he saw he'd gotten Eric's attention, he gestured at the heap of earth that had been uncovered from the shroud of fake green grass.

Time to finish this.

Eric took a handful of earth and tossed it down. Dark, thick clods scattered over the gleaming cherry-wood coffin that Maureen, Otis's sister-in-law, had selected. His brothers followed suit.

From the corner of his eye, he saw the guy with the greasy black hair and his thuggish pal stroll toward the access road where the mourners' cars were all parked. Good. He wouldn't have to wrangle Mace out of provoking them. He didn't have the juice for that fight today.

"Let's get the fuck out of here," Eric whispered to his brothers.

"Oh yeah," Mace agreed fervently.

They wasted no time putting distance between themselves and the rhythmic shovelfuls of dirt hitting Otis's coffin. They'd opted to park on the rough dirt road on the far side of the cemetery, far from the paved road where the mourners usually parked, for the purposes of a quick getaway. Why not avoid the stiff, awkward, socially mandated conversations from the get-go? They were doing everyone a favor by sparing them that necessity.

They were so intent on their escape, the black granite obelisk that loomed suddenly before th*em t*ook them by surprise. They all stopped in their tracks at the same moment.

Shit. Of all the fucking gravestones to stumble across today. It had been so long since he'd seen it, he'd somehow forgotten it was even here.

"Oh fuck." Mace cleared his throat. "That's just great. My cup runneth over."

They stood there like they'd all forgotten how to move, gazing at the list of names chiseled into the dark granite. Jeremiah Paley, 'The Prophet,' the charismatic leader of the survivalist compound where the three of them had grown up, topped the list. The rest of the adults that had died there followed him.

Nine children were listed at the end, in order of age.

Youngest last. Little Timothy Paley. Aged three years. Eric still remembered Timmy's high, squeaky voice.

The kids born up at GodsAcre had never had birth certificates. There were no documents to consult, no registries, no living adults with reliable information about the actual biological parentage or possible relatives of the smallest burned bodies.

Only Eric, Mace and Anton could bear witness to the fact that those little ones had ever existed at all. No one else on earth remembered them.

Those exclusive memories were a strange and heavy responsibility.

So they had all been listed as Paleys. Eric, Anton and Mace had been Paleys, too, having become Jeremiah's adopted sons after he had married their mother. They'd borne his name until Otis Trask adopted them, a year after the fire. When Otis had offered them his name, they'd jumped at the chance. A fresh start, not tethered to the past.

A memory floated up from Eric's mind as his eyes moved over the engraved inscription. Some church in town had got up a collection to buy a proper headstone for the victims of the fire and the minister had asked the three of them if there was anything special they wanted engraved on it.

Without thinking, Eric had blurted out a fragment of Jeremiah's favorite psalm. T*he Prophet had chanted it every time he got up in front of his congre*gation at GodsAcre.

He trains my hands for war so that my arms can bend a bow of bronze.

The Prophet never quite pulled that off, but it wasn't from lack of trying. Jeremiah had been crazy as all fuck, but no one could doubt the old man's commitment.

"Hey, you! Paley boys! Come to pay your respects to your psycho killer dad?"

They turned to see an older woman coming across the grass toward them. Her fuzzed gray hair was dragged back in an unkempt braid, and she wore a baggy sweat suit that had once been beige but was no longer. Her face looked caved in and her reddened eyes, sunk deep into bruised looking hollows, were wild and staring.

"No, ma'am," Eric said. "We're here for Otis's funeral. And our name is not Paley. We're Trasks now. Legally. For twelve years now."

"I don't give a shit what's on your driver's license." Her loud voice was slurred. "I know the truth. You can't bullshit me. I know what you are. You're garbage."

Eric waited for a careful, measured moment before replying. "Know whatever you want, ma'am," he said evenly. "And I'll do the same. Good afternoon."

But they weren't getting off that easy. The woman hustled toward them faster, a little unsteadily. Eric caught a scent of alcohol coming off her from yards away.

"You have nerve, coming here. See that grave?" She pointed behind herself, at a small headstone to the side of them. "That's my husband. My Malcolm. Do you know how he died? The Prophet's Curse, that's how. I put him in the ground and just a couple weeks later, the fucking bastard who murdered him gets buried right across from him.

Now I have to look at your killer dad's headstone every time I come to see Malcolm."

"He wasn't our dad." Mace's voice was flat. "He was our jailor."

"Bullshit. Garbage. Otis couldn't see the truth, but the rest of us did."

"Don't worry," Anton said. "We'll be out of your face soon. We won't be back."

"Bullshit. Liars. Just like the goddamn Prophet." Foamy spit dotted her purplish lips as she staggered closer.

Eric exchanged alarmed glances with his brothers. Jeremiah Paley's combat training had wired them up for lethal self-defense, but they had no playbook for drunken, unhinged female senior citizens on the rampage. They were on uncharted ground.

"Linda, that's enough." Wade Bristol's gruff voice sounded from behind them.

They turned to see the older man huffing up the slope, red faced. "You're not making sense," he scolded the woman. "These boys weren't responsible for Malcolm's death. They were just orphaned kids. Malcolm died of a stroke. You know that."

"Stroke, my ass! It was the curse!" Linda yelled. "Fourteen people in twelve days, Wade! And now Otis? He had a stroke, too! Just like Malcolm! It's starting up again, see? Now their own goddamn foster father is dead. Just like all the others. There's some fucking gratitude for you, eh?"

"Linda, calm down. They didn't have anything to do with—"

"Garbage!" she yelled. "They're garbage, and their fancy fucking suits can't change that!"

"Thank you, ma'am." Mace flicked an imaginary speck of lint from his lapel and adjusted his jacket on his broad shoulders. "Glad you like the threads at least."

"Shut up, Mace. You're not helping." Wade laid a soothing hand on Linda's shoulder. "Linda, calm down. Try to—"

"Go to hell." She flung off his hand and lurched back,

almost toppling over in the process. "All of you go to hell. Keep your murdering freak father company there."

They silently watched her totter down the grassy slope.

"You're not driving, are you, Linda?" Bristol called.

She flipped him off without turning. "Fuck you, Wade."

Wade cleared his throat self-consciously as Linda retreated. "Sorry about that."

"It's nothing we haven't heard before," Eric replied.

"Well, you shouldn't have to hear it the day you put Otis in the ground."

"Don't sweat it," Anton said. "At this point, we barely notice."

"Thanks for saving our asses, Chief Bristol," Mace said. "Nick of time, too. Don't know what we would have done. That dame woulda finished us."

The police chief gave him a quelling look. "Don't be a smart-ass. I buried a friend today, too, Mace, so shut your damn trap."

Mace's eyes went big and solemn. He made lip-zipping gesture.

Chief Bristol cleared his throat again and stuck his hand in his pockets. "So, ah…I just came over here to make sure you boys knew about the reception."

They looked at him blankly.

"Reception?" Eric repeated.

Chief Bristol grunted. "Figured as much. Since you don't answer calls and you came late to the funeral. And left before anyone could shake your hand or offer condolences."

"We don't have a lot to say to people here," Anton said. "What with one thing and another."

Bristol harrumphed. "That's a real unfortunate attitude."

"I guess it is." Anton's voice was unapologetic.

"Hmmph. Well." Chief Bristol's eyes went to Eric. "So I know we've had some tense moments in years past," he said. "I sure hope you won't hold it against me."

"I don't, Chief," Eric said. "It's all good. Past and gone."

Bristol looked cautiously relieved. "Well, that's fine, then. I think it would be a real good thing, a real appropriate thing, to go to that reception. For Otis's sake."

"Maureen didn't say anything about a reception," Eric said.

"Maureen didn't organize it," Bristol said. "There's a buffet spread at the Corner Café. You should drop by. Show some respect for the people who respected Otis. I'm heading over there now. I expect to see you there."

Eric stared after the man retreating back. Bristol's lecturing tone stuck in his craw, but he figured it came with the job. Otis had been a lecturer, too.

But Otis had worn authority far better than most.

They watched Bristol's big, unwieldy body stomping across the grass toward his pickup. When the vehicle was lost to sight in the trees, they turned to each other.

"Well, damn. That came out of nowhere," Anton commented.

"Yeah," Mace agreed. "Reception? What the fuck? Who's paying for it? Not Maureen, that's sure, the cheapskate bitch. She's still pissed that Otis left his house and land and truck to us instead of her two boys. She'll never forgive him for doing that."

"This morning, I gave her back the money she fronted for the funeral expenses," Eric said. "But she didn't mention anything about a reception."

"Probably didn't want us to come," Anton said. "Did she spit in your eye?"

Eric snorted. "Not until the check was in her purse."

Mace shook his head. "I'm not going to any goddamn reception, no matter what Chief Bristol says. I feel like hammered shit as it is. Why dial it up?"

"Agreed," Anton said. "I can only take this place in micro-doses. I blew over my safety limit a long time back."

Eric gave them a withering look. "Can't handle a little fish-eye? Pussies."

"Say whatever you want," Mason said. "You can't shame us into this."

"Fine," Eric said. "I'll stop in alone. Just long enough to reimburse whoever paid for it. I don't want to be indebted to anyone in this fucking place."

Mace snorted under his breath. "Why? We didn't organize it. I wouldn't voluntarily give the time of day to most of these people, much less cheese cubes and fruit skewers. After what all those pricks did to you seven years ago? Fuck 'em all sideways."

"Not an issue," Eric said, through his teeth. "Gone and forgotten."

"I doubt that the majority of the people at that reception will have forgotten it," Anton said. "I heard you say 'in and out and no drama.' But if you keep engaging with these people, you're going to generate some drama. It's a mathematical certainty."

"That's where you're wrong," Eric said. "I'm just going in to write a check. That gesture works on drama like a fire extinguisher. Poof, and everybody's smiling."

"You cynical bastard," Anton said. "And if Demi Vaughan is there, or her acid-spitting dad? I saw him staring at you from the minute you walked into the funeral home. A check isn't going to work on that guy's drama. He hates you so damn hard."

The look on Eric's face made Anton raise a cautious, soothing hand. "Easy," he said gently. "I couldn't help but notice that she was there. Right front and center. You noticed her, too. In a big, obvious way."

"That is a big affirmative," Mace chimed in. "Obvious as all fuck."

"Not. Relevant." Eric bit the words out through his teeth. "Ancient history."

Anton let out a sigh, a worried frown between his eyes. "If you say so."

But they didn't move. Both his brothers just stood there, staring at him with those worried, searching eyes until he wanted to smack the living shit out of them both.

"So?" he urged. "Get lost, you two. If you don't have the balls to go with me, then stop lecturing and let me get this over with."

"Watch yourself." Mace's voice was grim. "Remember what happened when you last had dealings with these people. It didn't end well. It almost destroyed you."

"It came out okay. I'm fine. She's fine. We all survived. We're different people now. Besides, she probably won't even be there. I'll just go say hello and thank you, write somebody a check and walk out. Clean slate. And we are done with this place."

"Okay," Anton said. "Happy cleaning. See you back at the ranch."

His brothers strode off toward Anton's gleaming Mercedes GLS. They got in and drove away without looking back at him. His brothers. Dragon-scale armored bad-asses. They always acted like they didn't give a shit. Never let anyone see behind their masks.

But he saw beneath it. Because he was just like them.

Otis's death had cut them all off at the knees. The old man had been like one of those volcanic granite monoliths that jutted up out of the turf like a preacher's pulpit. Weathering the storms, never changing, never giving any ground. A touchstone, a landmark. The most solid, reliable one that he'd ever had, other than Anton and Mace.

Otis hadn't been afraid of them. That had been the biggest gift that anyone could have possibly given them. It might have saved their lives.

He still remembered the day Otis had told them that the paperwork was ready if they wanted to take the Trask family name. He wanted to show his boys how a man stepped up and did the right thing. How he followed through on his word.

That gesture had been a big deal for them. A new name. A fresh start as a Trask.

Aw, shit. Thinking about that had messed him up. Now a big fist was squeezing his throat hard enough to crush it. The world had never felt particularly friendly to him, even at the best of times, but without Otis in it, it felt like a ticking bomb.

Which was exactly how Shaw's Crossing had seen him and his brothers.

To be fair, the townspeople had good reason to think it. With the intensive combat training they'd had since early childhood, he and Mace and Anton were fully as dangerous as the suspicious residents of Shaw's Crossing believed them to be. Probably more so.

But only Otis ever knew it for a fact, and Otis never told.

Old Jeremiah Paley had been a Vietnam vet. Delta Force. Trained to kill in every conceivable way. When he opened up

GodsAcre to true believers, he trained the children who lived there for war. After the Scourge, they were to be the vanguard of virtue in the blasted aftermath. The army of the faithful. It was a great responsibility which required expertise in small arms, knives, hand to hand, marksmanship, strategy, explosives, military history, guerilla warfare tactics. Jeremiah had been a relentless teacher, and Eric, Anton and Mace had been his best students.

Before he went entirely nuts. In that final, awful year when everything had gone to shit.

Eric was surprised as he drove through the downtown area of Shaw's Crossing on his way to the Corner Café to see how the business district had grown. It was trendy and touristy now. He parked his car a couple of blocks away from the café and strolled past a number of high-end shops, noticing sports gear, jewelry, crystal art, fancy housewares, a bookstore, an art gallery, coffee shops, a taco place. Sushi, even, for fuck's sake. Marconi's Corner Café diner used to be the only place downtown for food. If you could even call it food.

The Corner Café looked different, too. Its decaying fifties era vertical neon CAFÉ sign was gone, replaced by a big carved, painted wooden sign. The big picture windows that fronted both sides of the street corner were lavishly decorated with grease-pencil color drawings. Autumn leaves, pumpkins, a witch on a broomstick.

*It wa*sn't until he was right in front of the diner, in full sight of everyone crowded inside, that he focused on the words carved into the wooden sign.

Demi's Corner Café. The fuck?

Wade Bristol was inside, leaning over a buffet table. His face brightened when he saw Eric. He beckoned with a big hand piled with mini-burgers heaped on a napkin.

Benedict Vaughan saw him at the same moment, and choked on his wine. He grabbed a napkin from a napkin fan on the table, wiping his mouth, and flapped his hand at Eric in disgust. Shooing him off as if Eric were a raccoon knocking over garbage cans.

That fucking settled that. Eric pushed the door open and walked in.

Bristol lifted his glass to Eric. "Good to see you. Glad you decided to drop by. Anton and Mason chickened out, I take it?"

"You didn't tell me the Corner Café was Demi's." He could not control the accusatory tone that came out of his mouth.

"I'm surprised that Otis didn't tell you himself," Bristol said. "He loved eating here. The food is good. Much better than Ricky's ever was. Demi runs a tight ship. Great pie. And you need to talk to her anyhow."

"I do? Why?"

"She was the one who found Otis the other morning at his house. She was at the ICU with him when I showed up. And she was with him when he passed. She's also hosting this reception. All by herself. I just thought you should know."

Eric just stared at the police chief, his mind stalled out. "I, uh…didn't know."

"'Course not. How could you know? You've been too busy making sure nobody ever got a chance to talk to you."

Then Demi turned her head and met his eyes.

The contact zapped his mind blank, his mouth dry. She looked right inside him with those wide, light green eyes, as if he were made of clear glass. Everything lit up. In one swift, blazing assessment, she saw everything he was. Everything he'd ever been.

Everything he'd tried so hard forget.

---

**Available for preorder now! On sale February 21, 2020! https://shannonmckenna.com/books/headlong/**

**If you liked The Hellbound Brotherhood, lose yourself to passion and adventure in the world of The Obsidian Files! Turn the page and read the first chapter of Book One, Right Through Me. Available now!**

# RIGHT THROUGH ME
# THE OBSIDIAN FILES

***Stranger, speak softly...***

Biotech tycoon Noah Gallagher has a deadly secret: his clandestine training as a super-soldier gives him abilities that go far beyond human. Yet he's very much a man. When Caro Bishop shows up at his Seattle headquarters with a dangerous secret agenda, his ordered life is thrown into chaos. Caro is a woman like no other—and her luminously sensual beauty cloaks a mystery he must solve.

Caro's lying low, evading a false charge of murder. She means to clear her name, and she'll do whatever it takes to survive—but seducing a man like Noah is more than she bargained for. His amber eyes have the strangest glow when he looks at her—she could swear he sees the secrets of her heart. The desire smoldering in Noah's eyes awakens her own secret hunger, but Caro has to resist his magnetic pull. Anyone close to her becomes a target. The only right thing to do is run, far and fast, but Caro can't outrun Noah's ferocious intensity—or deny the searing passion that explodes between them.

Nothing else matters—until a vicious enemy bent on the ultimate revenge puts his murderous plan into play. Noah and Caro must battle for their lives...and their love...

**Turn the page for a taste of Right Through Me...**

# RIGHT THROUGH ME

## 1

Someone just cut the lights. What the hell?

Noah Gallagher put down his pen and looked around, startled, as drums began to thump from the hidden sound system of the penthouse conference room. Some exotic instrument joined in, throbbing and wailing.

The door to the conference room opened to a shimmery jingling sound, then a flash of fluttering purple. Everyone at the table was staring and murmuring.

Oh, Christ. Not possible. Noah rose to his feet, but the belly dancer was already halfway through the door, her hands weaving in a hypnotic pattern. Wide, light-catching green eyes laughed at him brazenly as she shimmied straight toward him, leading with one pulsing hip.

Her eyes caught him . . . and held him.

The world narrowed down. Whatever he was going to say or do stopped. Words were gone. Air was gone. Air didn't matter. Nothing moved while she moved.

She had commandeered all movement. With that smile.

Those eyes.

He was sitting again, with no memory of deciding to do so. His mind had gone blank. The woman was like a walking, breathing stun code, personally keyed to him. He'd always wondered how it would feel to be one of the unlucky chosen few at Midlands who'd gotten stun and kill codes embedded in their minds. His own brain implants had been bad enough. Stun and kill codes were worse.

But this dancer wasn't a goddamn stun code. She was just a random woman, shaking her stuff. When her act was done, he'd pull it together. Exert the fucking authority he was entitled to as the CEO of Angel Enterprises.

He had exactly until the music stopped to get control of himself.

Simple enough to figure out who'd dreamed up this unwanted birthday present. His younger sister Hannah lurked by the door. The wide-angle enhancement of his sight made it possible to see the gleam in Hannah's eyes without looking away from the belly dancer for a single second.

Not that he could have looked away.

He saw his fiancée Simone's face with his peripheral vision. She'd chosen to sit at his side for this important meeting. It was painfully obvious from her tight, expectant smile that she was waiting for him to turn to her, to smile and laugh and make light of this stupid situation. Not just for her. For everyone in the room.

He couldn't do it.

*Try. Do an analog dive. Grab a hook. Concentrate.*

A spotlight from somewhere gilded the dancer's body, highlighting every perfect detail. Silver anklets that jingled over her small, bare feet. Golden toenails. Shapely legs flashed between purple veils that floated from a low-slung, glittering belt. The belt and top were swagged with shining chains and dangling beadwork. Still more chains, draped from an ornate headdress, dangled over her forehead and under her chin, creating a constant soft shimmer of sound.

High, full breasts quivered, lovingly presented in the spangle-studded velvet bra. She arched back, floating a purple veil edged with spangles high in the air above herself and swishing her thick fall of of glossy black hair around. Had to be fake hair, falling to well below her ass. It brushed the curve of her hips. Fanned out as she twirled.

Everything he'd monitored in his peripheral vision was gone now. He no longer saw Hannah, or Simone, or anything else. His inner vision was too busy with the vivid fantasy of that woman straddling him. Imagining her bold, sensual smile as she swayed over him, teased him. Running her fingers through her hair, lifting it, tossing it. Coiling it around her waist like a slave rope.

He wanted to rip away all the filmy veils and all the goddamn beads and chains. See her bare-assed. Bare-breasted. Yeah.

The deep curve of her waist was perfectly shaped for his fingers to grip. The curves and hollows of her belly and her hips looked so soft. Touchable.

His hands shook with the urge to reach, stroke. Seize.

The rush of erotic images ramped up his advanced visual processor into screaming overdrive. Even with eyes shielded from eighty percent of the ambient light, even using a double layer of custom-designed shield specs, his AVP combat program was off and running, scrolling a thick column of data analysis past his inner eye.

And even that couldn't distract him from her show. Not for one instant.

His heightened senses reached out, so greedy for more that he found himself actually taking off the back-up shield specs. He'd have popped out the contacts, too, but his AVP was already going nuts at the lower protection level. Combine that with adrenaline, and a huge blast of sexual arousal—*fuck.*

The light level in this room could zap him into a stress flashback if he didn't protect his eyes. Not only that. The dark shield strength contact lenses hid the animal flash of amber luminosity caused by his visual implants. Outsiders couldn't be allowed to see that. The room was packed with outsiders. He wanted them gone.

Especially Simone. Which made him a total asshole. He tried hard, really hard, to feel guilty. Not so much as a twinge. His conscious mind had been almost totally hijacked by the dancer.

He wanted to throw everyone else out and lock the door. Study that woman with his naked eyes, dancing under the spotlight. But only for him. He wanted to gulp in the whole data flow. It was being filtered out in real time and lost to him forever, and it drove him . . . fucking . . . *nuts.*

And he couldn't do a thing. Not with an audience. His fists clenched in fury.

Heart racing, temperature spiking. Sweating profusely. No way to hide it. It was an AVP stress dump. A massive dose of fight-and-conquer energy, channeling straight into his dick, which strained desperately against his pants.

He struggled to grab onto the analog hooks that he'd established. His hooks were emergency mental shortcuts, activating an instant, deep withdrawal into the ice caves of his subconscious mind when the AVP got out of control. Best way he could devise to calm his stress reactions and stay on top of himself.

Not a hook to be had. Couldn't find them, couldn't feel them. Couldn't use his highly developed power of visualization at all, after years of grueling practice. All gone.

He was fully occupied imagining that woman naked and writhing beneath him.

His intense reaction to this spectacle made no sense. He'd seen belly dancing before and been unmoved. He did not have complicated fantasies or fetishes. He didn't even get the fun factor. He wasn't known for his sense of humor. In fact, he had no imagination at all, unless you counted biotech engineering designs, or plotting ways to grow his business, or scheming to keep his chosen family alive, secret, and safe.

That demanding enterprise left no bandwidth for fun and games.

He wasn't playful about sex, either. He was tireless, focused. Relentless in making sure that his partners were satisfied. To the point of exhaustion, even. Theirs, not his. They would tell him he was the hottest lover ever and then call him cold.

So? Noah didn't do emotions. Cold was safer for everyone concerned.

Not that he could explain that to whoever happened to be in bed with him.

He couldn't change his nature. He saw to it that his lovers had many orgasms to his one, to compensate for those mysterious intangibles. Whatever the fuck else they wanted from him, it just wasn't there. He didn't even know where to look for it.

The dancer's arms lifted, swayed. He inhaled the scent of her dewy skin as she spun closer. Fresh, sweet, hot. Sun on the flowers. Rain on the grass. His mouth watered.

Since what happened at Midlands, his senses were

sharper than normal by many orders of magnitude. He had ways to blunt the overload, but not this time. He was catching a full data load now, shields and all. Tripping out on her undulating hand movements.

He was reading her energy signature, right through the shield lenses. A cloud of hot, brilliant colors surrounded her. Her floating purple veils blended with trailing clouds of her body's energy, to which his AVP overstimulated brain assigned all the colors of the spectrum and more besides. Colors not visible to anyone but him.

Along with it a strange sensation was growing. Tension, anticipation. Dread.

He was used to being alone in an insulated bubble. Other people's drama raged outside that protective barrier and left him completely untouched. He needed it that way to stay in control. Maintaining isolation required constant effort and vigilance.

Now, suddenly, he wasn't alone. The girl had danced through his force field. Invaded his inner space. It was messy and crowded in there now.

She took up room. Confused him with her colors, her scents. Her smile was so unforced and sensual. She was bonelessly flexible, yet still regal in her diaphanous veils.

It made him jittery to have someone so close. The intimacy felt awkward. Ticklish.

He felt hot, red. No control over his face. Stuck here, sitting among colleagues and family, right next to his fiancée. Any one of them could watch him watch her. At least the massive conference table concealed his colossal hard-on.

He had not felt this helpless since Midlands.

Her luminous green eyes met his and then flicked away, but the electric buzz of that split instant of intimacy jolted him to depths he'd never felt before.

He knew he'd never seen this woman before, and yet he recognized her.

---

Caro narrowly missed slamming her hip into the table. For the third time.

*Look away from the guy, for God's sake. Get a grip. It's just a dance.*

But her gaze kept getting sucked back to Noah Gallagher, the birthday boy. Ultra-powerful CEO of the oh-so-mysterious Angel Enterprises, cutting-edge biotech firm.

The man was gorgeous. Barrel chested. A dense slab of muscle. Short hair showed off the sharp planes and angles of his face, a wide, strong jaw. He wore shaded glasses, but he'd taken them off a few seconds into her dance. It was incredibly hard to stay focused on the music and remember her moves while being examined with such blazing intensity. It wiped her mind blank. Made her lose the thread.

To say nothing of her physical balance.

Holy flipping *wow.* They said he was turning thirty-two today, but he seemed older, or maybe it was just his expression. Each time she twirled, she snagged a new yummy detail. The shape of his ears. Thick, straight dark brows. Sexy grooves framing a stern but still sensual mouth. Sharp cheekbones. His face was a taut mask of tension, as if he were suppressing strong emotion. But it was his eyes that really got to her.

His scorching laser focus made her temperature rise. She'd always been sensitive to the quality of a person's energy. Noah Gallagher's energy dominated the room. He looked like he'd tear you to pieces if you gave him any trouble, despite the elegant suit that sat just right on his huge shoulders. He didn't laugh or look embarrassed like most men did when surprised by a belly dancer. He just sat there, with the charged stillness of a predator poised to spring. Radiating danger.

Her smile faltered as she shimmied and spun. Suddenly, she was hyper-conscious of the erotic allure of the dance. His silent, very male sexual energy made it feel deadly serious. As if they were alone, and she'd been summoned for a private, uninhibited performance designed to drive him crazy.

Oh my. What a stimulating scenario.

She was actually getting aroused. For the love of God. Rising panic began to shred the sensation. Enough of this ridiculous crap. She had to get out of here, and fast.

*Finish the dance. You need the cash. He's only a hot guy, not a celestial being. You're freaking yourself out. Chill.* Usually she spread the wealth, bestowing flirtatious smiles on everyone. Not tonight. They weren't feeling it. Young men were usually always enthusiastic, and there were several of them here, but no one made a sound. Tension was thick in the air. No laughter, no snickering, no whistles.

Who cared. Her mind was fully occupied with the task of not gaping at Noah Gallagher's godlike hotness. Being aware of every inch of skin she displayed to him.

Her gaze bounced across the blond woman who sat next to him. A little younger, but not a colleague or an assistant. They sat too close together for that. The woman's mouth looked tight and miserable. Next to her sat a flushed, heavy older man who stared fixedly at Caro's beaded bra, nostrils flared.

*Rise up, cupcake. Take back the power.* This was a tough crowd, maybe, but everything was relative. The people in this room weren't trying to frame her for murder, kidnap her or kill her. And she certainly had the birthday boy's full attention.

So she'd play with it. What the fucking hell. That man needed to be humbled. To worship at the feet of her divine awesomeness. She'd dance like she'd never danced before, blow his mind, and melt away, forever nameless. Leaving him to ache and writhe.

*That's right, big boy. Prepare to suffer.*

But Noah Gallagher's fierce, unwavering gaze was having a strange effect on her. Ever since she'd gone into hiding, she'd had a sick, heavy lump in her belly. For months it had been sitting there, like a chunk of dirty ice that would not melt. But when she looked at him, that pinched coldness eased. It turned soft and warm and alive.

It felt amazingly good. Dancing for him, she could actually breathe again.

For as long it lasted.

The dance was ending. Caro sank to her knees, arching back in a pose of abandoned sensual ecstasy as the music reached its climax, luxurious fake hair brushing the ground in her grand finale. Dancing had never made her feel so naked before. She was stretched before him like a sacrificial virgin on an altar.

*Take me.*

The pose felt obscene, but only because there were other people in the room. If there hadn't been, it would have felt right. It would have felt . . . *hot.*

The sound of one person frantically clapping broke the silence. Hannah Gallagher, the girl who had hired her. Noah Gallagher's younger sister, from the looks of her. Caro rose slowly to her feet. Noah Gallagher didn't applaud. He just stared at her, as if he wanted to leap over that table and pin her down.

Tension built like an electrical charge. The other people in the room looked up, down, anywhere but at her. Caro smiled brightly. Held her head as high as possible.

Not fair, to throw a paid performer into the middle of someone else's big fat faux pas and make her swim in it. Bastards.

"That was fabulous!" Hannah's voice was a little too high. "Thanks for a gorgeous dance, Shamira! Happy birthday, Noah! Wasn't she awesome, everyone?"

Not one yes. There was only dead silence, downcast eyes, awkward looks exchanged all around. And still, Noah Gallagher's devouring eyes.

So what. She'd stay dignified. While running for her life, fighting the powers of darkness, scrambling for money. Even if it involved putting on a scanty costume and shaking her booty for rude or indifferent strangers.

Or, in this case, one single intense, lustful, smoldering stranger.

She took a slow, deliberate bow, as if she were in front of an adoring crowd. Taking her own sweet time. Rubbing their faces in it.

*Take that, you rude shitheads. Like it would kill you to clap.*

She didn't need any validation from these self-important bio-tech-nerd idiots. Just her fee, which she would get whether they liked her performance or not.

Fuck 'em. She had things to do. Important things. After one more hungry peek at the mouthwatering godking. Lord, he was fine.

She flash-memorized him in one breathless instant, whipping her gaze away from his face before eye contact could start the inevitable sexual mind-melt reaction. Then she swept out of the room, chin up, shoulders back. A regal sweep of purple veils.

That was it. She would never see him again. She wasn't going to feel that hot rush of opening in her chest, ever again.

*Suck it up. Ignore the lust buzz. Sport sex is reserved for normal people. Fugitives do without. And don't whine.*

Hannah followed her out of the room, and slammed the door harder than was necessary. "You were gorgeous," she said fervently. "You're so talented. I'm so sorry they didn't clap or anything. I'm going to tell them all off. Noah will kill me, but I'm used to it."

"I'll rather not watch that," Caro said hastily. "I'll just be on my way."

"Oh no! Stay just a minute! You have to at least say hi to Noah. No matter what he says to me, he certainly enjoyed your dance. I'm the villain here. You're just an innocent bystander. Noah's very fair that way. And I'm sure he'll want to meet you!"

*In your dreams, honey.* "Let me, ah, change first," Caro said, backing away.

"You remember the way to the office? Come back after. I'll introduce you."

The door flew open. A man strode out, not the birthday boy. This one was tall, blue eyed and very built, his thick dark blond hair hanging down to his shoulders. His eyes flicked over her with controlled curiosity and then turned back to Hannah.

"What the *hell* were you thinking?" he asked.

Definitely her cue. Caro took off, hurrying back toward the nondescript office that'd served as a dressing room. She didn't even want to know what Hannah's answer might be.

Not her family, not her fight.

Once inside the empty office, she could still hear them arguing from behind the door. Other people had gotten into the mix. Voices were being raised. Her heart pounded as she peeled off her costume and packed it up. She pulled on her shapeless street clothing, trying not to overhear. She had her own problems. Big nasty ones. Time to cruise discreetly away and let them get on with theirs.

Makeup pads got most of the paint off. She rolled the expensive dancing wig into its carrying bag, and put on her street wig, a thick brown bob with heavy bangs and wisps curling in around her face to conceal its shape. When she arrived, she hadn't worn the mouth prosthesis, which puffed out her cheeks and distorted her jawline. She'd figured that the coat and hat were enough weirdness for the client to swallow. But the job was done, and she hoped to God she could slink out unnoticed, so in went the mouth thing. Big tinted glasses finished the look, topped off by her hat with LED lights in the brim, ordered off the Internet to foil facial recognition software her pursuers might use to find her on social media.

Who knew if it really worked. At least the wide brim kept the Seattle drizzle off.

Her hands still shook as she pulled on her oversized black wool coat. The foam lining she'd sewn in bulked up her shoulders and hips. She looked sixty pounds heavier, and slightly humped.

At first, she'd tried changing the way she moved as part of her disguise, but after all the bodywork she'd done in college, she decided that the psychological toll of slumping and shuffling was dangerous to her soul. Inside her frumpy cocoon of foam and wool, she still had her pride and attitude.

Hidden, maybe, but structurally intact.

When she exited the office, she looked like a sketch that had been blurred on purpose. Noah Gallagher would stare right through her even if she were inches away.

That thought was so depressing, she could barely stand to think it.

*Chin up.* She'd had her fun, turning him on. Time for the disappearing act. Eat your heart out, Laser Eyes.

But disappearing didn't feel powerful to her. It just felt flat. Empty and sad.

The route back to the elevators took her right past the conference room.

Hannah Gallagher and several others were still arguing outside it. If she kept her head down, turned the corner and cut swiftly across the open space, she'd only be in their line of vision for a few seconds. Then it was a straight shot to the elevator.

One, two . . . *go.*

When she was squarely in the danger spot, Noah Gallagher came out the door.

That was her undoing. She slowed down. Not consciously, but simply unable to resist the temptation to steal one last look at him before fleeing.

His gaze snapped onto her, like a powerful magnet coupling.

Oh, God. Oh, no. He strode through the center of the group, scattering them, and followed her. Even with her back to him, his eyes burned through her layered, ugly disguise, a focused point of heat against her concealed skin. She stabbed the elevator button. He was twenty yards away. Fifteen, and closing. Picking up speed.

He couldn't have recognized her. In this dreary get-up,

she couldn't be more different from Shamira the sexy dancing girl. She barely recognized herself dressed like this. The door slid open. She lunged inside. No other riders, thank God.

"Hold the door!" Gallagher called, loping for the elevator.

Asfuckingif. She punched the close button, and the mechanism engaged.

Their eyes locked, as the doors shut in his face.

Her heart was thudding, as if she'd done something wrong and had almost gotten caught. Maybe he was just wondering who the scruffy stranger was. Dressed like that, she stuck out like a sore thumb in the muted corporate elegance of Angel Enterprises.

She hurried through the lavish front lobby. Outside, a cab was letting a passenger out. She bolted for it, waving it down.

Noah Gallagher emerged from the entrance just as her cab pulled away. His eyes locked onto hers again instantly. Even shadowed by the hat, obscured by the dark glasses, through the back window of a cab that was already a half a block away.

He started running after her. Right out onto the street. Eyes still locked. The contact felt like a wire, pulling tighter and tighter. Then the taxi turned a corner and he was lost to sight. It hurt. As if something vital had been snipped with bolt-cutters.

Her fizz of excitement died away. The cold lump of fear was back in place.

She was so sick of feeling this way. She wanted to yell at the driver to circle the block, just on the off chance of catching one last glimpse of Noah Gallagher. To feel something different than that cold, heavy ache in her core. Just for a second or two.

But she could not have this. Not even a stolen taste of it. She could not let lust trash her good judgment. She had to stay murderously sharp. Constantly on the defensive. Without rest.

Sexual frustration wouldn't kill her.

But there were other things out there that definitely could.

**Join Shannon's newsletter mailing list to never miss a new book or a fabulous promo, and look for your free gift book when you join!**

**http://shannonmckenna.com/connect.php.**

**Follow her on Bookbub to receive new release and discount alerts!**

**https://www.bookbub.com/authors/shannon-mckenna**

# ABOUT THE AUTHOR

Shannon McKenna is the NYT and USA TODAY bestselling author of over twenty action packed, turbocharged romantic thrillers, among them the wildly popular McCloud Brothers & Friends Series, along with two new scorching romantic suspense series, The Hellbound Brotherhood and The Obsidian Files. She loves tough and heroic alpha males, heroines with the brains and guts to match them, terrifying villains who challenge them to their utmost, adventure, blazing sensuality, and most of all, the redemptive power of true love. Since she was small she has loved abandoning herself to the magic of a good book, and her fond childhood fantasy was that writing would be just like that but with the added benefit of being able to take credit for the story at the end. The alchemy of writing turned out to be messier than she'd ever dreamed, but what the hell, she loves it anyway and hopes that readers enjoy the results of her experiments. She loves to hear from her readers. Contact her at her website, http://shannonmckenna.com, find her on Facebook at https://www.facebook.com/AuthorShannonMckenna/ to keep up with all her news! Follow her on Bookbub to get new release and discount alerts!

https://www.bookbub.com/authors/shannon-mckenna

If you'd like to know when the new installments of The Hellbound Brotherhood will come out, and hear about my new releases and promos, join my newsletter at http://shannonmckenna.com/connect.php.

I'll give you an Obsidian Files novel as a welcome gift! See you on the other side!